*This Book Is Dedicated To my Family*

# Table of Contents

History 1 – Beginning 1

History 2 – Back in the Cad 11

History 3 – Where is Stinson Beach 23

History 4 – In Stinson Beach City 37

History 5 – Tired 53

History 6 – Day Eight 69

History 7 – Fran glad to see me 79

History 8 – Day Eleven 89

History 9 – Children 99

History 10 – Day Twenty One 109

History 11 – At the Hippo 127

History 12 – Police Stopped Me 139

History 13 – Best Friend Jerry 151

History 14 – C-Note 161

History 15 – After five year 175

# History 1

# "Beginning"

San Francisco is always up to something and this night she was up to her bare butt in oil. Crude oil that is - all over the damn beautiful bay. Two Standard Oil Company tankers collided in the early morning and spilled their guts of dull black, jelly-like crude oil. The oil moved inexorably onto beaches at Half Moon Bay, San Francisco and the entire perimeter surrounding Oakland and Richmond. The heaviest oil concentrations were in the vicinity of Alcatraz and the south side of Angel Island.

Through television and radio airwaves, the news of the collision and spill spread quickly. "Due to dense fog, the collision of two sister ships, the inbound Arizona Standard and the outbound Oregon Standard, took place at 1:42 a.m., January 18, 1971, causing the Oregon Standard's load of bunker fuel - an estimated twenty thousand barrels of the total - to pour onto the shores of San Francisco Bay and the California coast."

In the dead of the night, the oil spill caused immediate destruction to the sea life. Fish swam into a black rubbery door that inhibited their breathing. Seagulls dove for food and couldn't emerge because the oil pulled them down like animals stuck in quicksand. Sea animals began washing up on the shores struggling, panicking and gasping for air to stay alive only to die seconds later.

A dark cloud covered the moon and the air smelled of tar. The fog was wet and moist like a light drizzle. People taking strolls during the night had problems breathing as they caught wind of the foul air. By dawn, Standard Oil Company executives, supervisors and managers had for several hours been frantically trying to hire everyone they could to help clean up the oil spill. They spent the entire day trying to organize cleanup and sea life rescue efforts. While Standard Oil executives were trying to hire every trucker in the world, I returned from a family trip to Memphis and spent the day planning a dinner party for all of my employees to celebrate my newfound success in the trucking industry under my company, Walker Trucking.

After planning during the day, I partied all through the night, only stopping once at the club, which by law, closed at 2 a.m.. My three-piece suit was the perfect attire. While I was partying, the world went on without me. After the party, I drove around trying to hook up with one of my female sports. However, after two failed attempts, I decided to take my butt home to my wife, Ann, and my three young daughters: Yolanda, Charlette (Dee Dee) and Ruedell (Pookie). As time was sneaking up on 4 a.m., January 19, 1971, I was in the slow lane winding my way home in my new gold and black Cadillac.

The interior still had the fresh smell of leather. I was tired but overpowered with the thrill of my Cadillac, which intrigued me. I smiled with a cynical grin thinking, *"Hell, even my car is paid for!"* As I relaxed into the seat a little more, I reflected on how successful I was - especially for a nigga livin' in Hunters Point. On the legal side, I had six dump trucks hauling dirt from a construction site of the Bay Area Rapid Transit (BART).

My contract was under Chet C. Smith Trucking - the company owned by the same man who swore he'd never hire a black. However, after I got nationwide coverage from a dramatic one-man demonstration that stopped construction on an underground section

2

of BART, white contractors were forced by BART to hire me and every other black trucker with a rig that wanted in. This also gave me membership to the "Club." Belonging to the "Club" meant that my cartooned picture hung on the wall of Bruno's Restaurant on Mission Street in San Francisco along with all the white contractors and big shots of the San Francisco building and construction trades. So with a steady profit coming in and having helped the "Brothers," I deserved living good and that was all I wanted. Besides, the news coverage made me a "Black Hero" in the community I loved, my home in Hunters Point. I was asked to speak at various functions and my advice on a number of unrelated subjects was highly sought after.

I was approaching the Fell Street exit. When I got off the freeway, I stopped for a red light. A little farther up the street, while passing through the intersection of Webster and Fell, I couldn't believe my eyes. My instinct alarm went off as I watched twenty empty dump trucks with white drivers roar by in a convoy. Instantly I was alert. I immediately shook the lingering party mentality that I was in and became attentive to what was happening.

Pulling myself up straight in the seat, I muttered to myself, "Son-of-a-bitch. Working at night? These white motherfuckers must have a secret agenda. They're sneakin' around in the dark so they can keep the black truckers out."

When the light changed, I heavily pressed the gas pedal, turning to follow them. I remembered how tired I'd felt a moment before and how nice it would be to sleep. But I was wired now and back in the game. I knew the game demanded a price and the price that it demanded this morning was for me to somehow ignore the fact that my body was spent. "Fuck it," I muttered with determination, "I'm gonna follow these bastards and find out what they're up to."

I was two blocks from the freeway off-ramp at Fell and Laguna when out of nowhere a line of eighteen-wheelers and dump trucks appeared in front of me. Each lane was occupied.

Night work had been rare, but several factors could have been involved. Perhaps they were getting an early start to travel to a distant location for work, perhaps a trucking contractor was moving his motor pool to a new yard or maybe they were lost and took the wrong off-ramp. However, I spotted a familiar face. The face I recognized was Billy's and I knew Billy wasn't lost. Billy taught me how to take care of my trucks. He was a conscientious white boy and I never recognized a racist mood swing in him. I knew he was competent and grounded. He was on a mission.

All of a sudden, my curiosity peaked and my adrenaline began to flow. I thought, *"What the fuck is going on? Where are those motherfuckas going? I'm joining this parade."* Two business alliances, if you could call them that, Chet Smith and Ralph Rogers, as the trucks clearly depicted their names, owners of the two largest trucking companies in the Bay Area, were now on the move at night.

"Niggers sleep at night," a white fellow told me Ralph said; "all but Charlie." I glanced in the back seat where my hard hat always lay. It was there. A broad smile came over my face because I was about to bust their butts. For no apparent reason other than their preference in skin color, Chet and Ralph thought that only white truckers should haul.

The excitement about black truckers finally getting work had calmed down because everyone, black and white, was working. Regardless of the excitement or attention the situation garnered, I was proud that I had made a contribution to the black cause.

At one point during my incessant pursuit of the convoy, I thought, *"This could wait until morning, but hell, I'm going to pursue this anyway. I'll just find the location, see what's happening, compile my data, call them tomorrow and listen to them lie."* Chet was an obvious liar.

One day as we were just kicking back and relaxing, Chet said, "I never lie, I just tell my side." I guess I was somewhat like that too. As I attempted to line up behind the last truck, I could not

4

help but wonder where they were going. When I reached the top of Steiner and Fell, I stopped for the red light. I glanced into my rearview mirror and could see all the vehicles coming off the freeway. Every lane was filled with trucks. *"What the fuck?!"* I thought. I had never seen so many trucks at one time.

Before I could reach the rear of the caravan, about fifty tractors and trailers passed by me. As I pulled to the right, I was approaching Divisadero Street when motorcycle police passed me with their red lights flashing and sirens blasting. *"My, my, my,"* I said to myself, *"what have we here?"*

They were heading in the direction of Golden Gate Park. I knew of no new hauling jobs in that area. I was right behind them by the time they turned left off Fell Street and onto Lincoln Way, which led through the Panhandle of Golden Gate Park. We drove past 2nd Avenue all the way down to 19th Avenue. Once again, I glanced into my rearview mirror and could see more trucks were approaching. Official vehicles were flying by me.

Motorcycle police and squad cars started blocking off intersections. Police were coming from all directions. With police escorts, the trucks were picking up speed. "Ah crap, this is taking too long," I thought aloud. "I'm too tired. I'll find out tomorrow." I was beginning to doubt my instincts.

Just then, I came to a "No Left Turn" sign, but I was determined to make that left turn until I saw a motorcycle cop sitting at the curb looking right at me. I continued driving straight for the next three blocks because I couldn't make a left turn and the streets were blocked with construction. "What the hell, I may as well check it out tonight," I finally concluded.

A couple of times I was motioned by the police to get out of the caravan, but I knew how to play this game. I reached over in the back seat, picked up my hard hat, put it on and re-entered the "parade." As I passed 35th Avenue, I could see in the distance that the whole area was lit up! *"What the hell is going on?"* I wondered.

5

I realized at that point I had not turned on the radio all day and in fact, had not looked at television either. Usually, if a tragedy occurred, the newspapers on the corner would have the headlines printed in big bold letters. I didn't even remember having seen a newspaper that day.

What could have possibly happened? As I turned on the radio, I was approaching 48th Avenue. As far as I could see, there were trucks and police on motorcycles, on horseback and in squad cars. In the background was the Pacific Ocean, calm and peaceful.

There must have been two hundred trucks parked and from a distance everything seemed especially tranquil. About four to six blocks later, I was in the midst of glaring makeshift lights and a horde of construction types were scurrying around under them. Heightened with curiosity, I nosed the Cadillac right in like I was in charge. I then turned the engine off and got out of the car.

I realized that I was standing in the huge parking lot of San Francisco's Ocean Beach. Still dressed in a three-piece suit, I strutted around like a supervisor. A moment later, my tired eyes caught sight of none other than Chet Smith. In earlier times we had gone from fierce enemies to good business friends, or so I thought.

Chet was with his usual flunkies standing around him, all of them chewing tobacco. I immediately had to get on stage with my hard hat in place, eyes tight, teeth gritted, tough guy attitude, while being casual and strolling along as if I knew what was happening. Chet saw me. He looked as if he had not slept in a week.

His eyes were saying, "What in the hell is he doing here?" A person's eyes told me most of what I wanted to know about them. I couldn't remember when I had been wrong. I read expressions, lip movements and any nervous conditions. It was necessary for businessmen to possess that ability and it was also imperative that a salesman could read a face.

Wrinkles started to appear on the side of Chet's eyes. White businessmen had a talent that most black men had not acquired, an

6

"I hate you" smile. However, I knew it on sight and all good businessmen knew it and had it. "I should have known," I said to the salty air. When I got a few yards closer, Chet had regained his composure. I instantly said, "What the fuck's going on Chester? You sons-of-bitches pullin' another fast one on me, huh?"

"Hey Charlie, I was just going to call you!" he yelled back as he waved and lumbered his six-foot, two-inch frame, which matched mine, toward me while smiling with a big hand stuck out in front of him.

We shook hands and he slapped me on the back while I chided, "Don't give me that shit, Chester. You know that you're a greedy bastard. You're busy this late at night so that you can hoard more money." He chuckled as I tried to see beyond the glare of the lights and all the equipment. Waving my hand at the confusion, I asked, "Looks like a damn ant hill. What the hell is going on here anyway?"

"We're cleaning up part of that quarter of a million barrels of crude oil that's washing up on the beach. Standard Oil is trying to round up every truck this side of Reno to help haul off the mess. Hell, BART's all but shut down because all the trucks used for hauling are here."

So that was it. My mind began to tabulate the chain reaction right down to actual dollars for hauling off the mess and getting the giant of giants, Standard Oil, out of a bind."When did this happen?" I asked. Chet answered, "Just before dawn yesterday morning, I think." I replied, "Good, that means lots of confusion. Confusion means quick decisions and lots of profits."

Adrenaline was quickening my pulse as I thought of the opportunity that would quickly be gone. "Charlie," Chet said.

"Chet," I replied as I returned my "I hate you also" smile. "Charlie, where have you been?" "Nowhere, Chet." "I heard you were out of town." "You can't believe everything you hear, Chet." "I have been trying to reach you." "I am sure you have." Both of us looked at each other. Chet knew I knew he was lying.

7

However, he wasn't really lying! He was just telling me his side of it.

"Charlie, Standard Oil has really got a mess on their hands." I thought to myself, "What mess?" Chet continued, "Contractors are talking to several of the big wheels from Standard Oil. They are trying to explain how we are going to get up all the oil that they spilled in the Bay Sunday night."

I retorted, "I knew you knew what had happened. Otherwise, how did you know it was an accident?" What Chet didn't understand was that I just said "accident" by accident. Chet replied, "I knew you didn't know anything about anything. That is why you are looking in my face now." We both laughed.

Stepping a little closer to Chet, I reached and touched him on the arm attempting to punctuate the sincerity of my position. "I want in Chet. How do I get a contract on this thing?" He looked at me as if I was crazy, but held his tongue and instead lifted his hard hat with one hand and ran his fingers through his distinguished, graying hair. For an instant he glanced in the direction of the noise coming from the equipment and men.

Then his gaze returned to me with his forehead wrinkled and his face taut. He said, "Charlie, this is a big one. I don't know how much I can be of assistance to you but I'll tell you the little bit that I know." Sensing some advantage, I felt pleasure. I liked it when someone underestimated me; it gave me an edge.

"Fuck all that. How can I get a piece of the action, Chet?" "All the hiring is taking place at the Long Wharf in Richmond. Shit, Charlie, I don't know if you can get in; every contractor around is already there trying to get a piece. But if you want to give it a shot, they're signing up people over at the Long Wharf." "Chet, don't bullshit me."

"You know I wouldn't bullshit you, Charlie. The same hour the ships collided, I got a call from a contractor named Marshall Munzer telling me about Standard Oil's intentions. He had heard about it on the radio and I saw some of it on TV, so I went over there yesterday morning and offered my trucks to help with the efforts. "I'll bet that if you go over there, they will give you a small beach to clean up."

"Yeah, and maybe it will be in downtown San Francisco."

As he stared into my eyes, I could see through him; all he wanted was to get rid of me. Around this time, the press and a very tall, thin, middle-aged man walked over to where we were standing. On his lapel a nametag announced, "Mr. Smith."

"Smith!" he said in a commanding voice. "We have got to thin these trucks out. Send some of them down the Great Highway." Chet said, "Excuse me, Charlie. Good luck! I would take a look if I were you." I said, "Okay. I'll let you know what happens."

I walked up to Mr. Smith. His hard hat also had "Smith, Field Supervisor" written distinctly on it.

"Pardon me, Mr. Smith. Do you think Standard Oil can use some more help?" He replied, "I am sure we can use every available truck and field supervisor." "All the hiring is at the Long Wharf?" "That's right," he replied. Chet was out of earshot, so I said, "Mr. Smith, Chet informed me of the same. However, he said to speak to you before I go to the Long Wharf." He had just seen me talking to Chet. He said, "Here is my card. Tell the people over there what you have in line of equipment and if they are still in need I am sure they will give you something to clean up. Now if you'll excuse me, I have to get back to work."

Before I could ask any more questions, he quickly turned and walked away. As he moved away I yelled, "Thanks." Never completely stopping, he turned and waved. Now I knew there was a real chance for me. I thought about what Chet had said and knew that he meant the refinery in Richmond, which was right across the Richmond Bridge from San Quentin. "Well I'd better hurry then," I said as I spun around and quick-stepped toward the car. A plan was already forming and I knew I might need Chet's help if it worked.

9

# History 2

# "Back in the Cad"

Climbing back in the Cad, I pointed it in the direction of Richmond. The sun was coming up and my body, which was already spent, was now dragging as I drove across the Bay Bridge. The game was on and my chance to be in it would be over in a few hours. I forced myself to stay awake.

I turned around and started back down Lincoln Way, the first street in the inner and outer Sunset District. More people lived in that area of San Francisco than in any other. It was a showplace for Victorian homes. After the 1906 earthquake, the inner and outer Sunset District was built on sand dunes, which were made of dirt and hard clay. Plants couldn't easily grow because of the hard soil. Dirt was imported to make the land sturdier before contractors built affordable homes. Since there was such little property space, row houses were built. They had beautiful bay windows that faced Golden Gate Park and displayed the main room of the house. The homes were made primarily of brick and painted pastel colors because the sun easily faded dark colors.

Different varieties of trees like the cottonwood and pine were imported to aesthetically enhance the area and because they needed little water. The redwoods were also imported because they grew well on the hard clay.

Lincoln Way was parallel to Golden Gate Park, one of the

largest manmade parks in California. Golden Gate Park bordered one side of Lincoln Way and filled the air with a strong sap aroma. There were museums, Japanese gardens, flower houses, buffalo, various species of reptiles, serene horseback riding trails and jogging lands - it was the perfect place to go and relax. Lincoln Way curved around and turned into Oak Street. From Oak Street, any highway was accessible, but it led directly to the Bay Bridge.

As I made my way across the Bay Bridge, day broke. The air was so fresh that I could taste it. By now, I was wide awake. The radio was filling me in on what had happened. "Two Standard Oil Company tankers collided off the Golden Gate Bridge early yesterday and floated into the bay, one of them dumping over a half-million gallons of heavy, gooey bunker oil into the Bay - the biggest recorded spill in its history. The Arizona Standard's bow collided with the port side of the Oregon Standard, just off the Oregon's bow, ripping a hole sixty-five feet long and thirty to forty feet deep and rupturing at least two of the ship's twenty-six oil-containing compartments.

"The Oregon Standard was heading for British Columbia containing 106,000 barrels of bunker fuel. A barrel contains forty-two gallons. The Arizona Standard was inbound from Estero Bay, near San Luis Obispo, with 115,000 barrels of crude oil. None of her oil was spilled. Both tankers, 523 feet and 17,000 ton vessels, were moving in a fog that cut visibility almost to zero."

All the windows were down and my whole body seemed to inhale the brisk air. Wearing a hard hat and a well-tailored suit, I felt like success, but most importantly, I felt that if there was one job left when I got on this Long Wharf office or in it, I was going to get some of it.

As I made my way around the edge of the Bay, there were mountains that stood like a forest of trees for miles. After leaving the beautiful San Francisco-Oakland Bay Bridge, I passed the border of several little communities, such as Emeryville, Albany and Berkeley. Most of the time, my front wheels were in one little city and my rear wheels in another. In fifteen minutes, I was approaching the Standard Oil refinery. I knew I was in the right place because I could see the smokestacks.

After rounding Cutting Boulevard, it was straight ahead - Standard Oil. I could see three tanker trucks were approaching the front gates. As I rounded the corner, I was directly behind the last tanker and the first sign I saw said, "No Admittance. No Private Vehicles. No Open Flames." No this, no that, and, most daunting, "No Help Wanted." I laughed. If they didn't need any help, why was I there?

I didn't really know why I was over there. It was so unlikely that those people were going to hire me. I knew that the next day I was going to look at myself in the mirror and say, *"Were you crazy? You didn't know anything about oil except that it goes in a car or truck."*

It seemed that something was pushing me to keep going and I had no control over my actions. In retrospect, that morning I did several things that were out of character. It was unusual for me to just drive around alone late at night or for me to take someone's word without any proof, as I had by listening to Chet and Mr. Smith; however reasonable it sounded, they could be sending me off on a wild goose chase.

As I neared the Standard Oil domain of wharves, ships and warehouses, huge round gray tanks filled with black money dominated my view. It was about 6:30 a.m.. My radio informed me that the newspapers, radio and television stations, politicians and "Joe Public" had been attacking Standard Oil. To add insult to injury, even at such an early hour college kids were picketing in front of the gate. I thought, *"What the fuck are all these teenagers doing here so early in the morning?"* I pulled up close behind the last tanker. I was so far back that I initially could not see anyone at the entrance.

I pulled over to the side to see what was going on at the front gates. I saw a barricade of police officers and cars parked on the outside of the Standard Oil fence - Richmond police, Standard Oil Security and the Pinkerton Protective Agency. There were seventy-five gun-toting fools!

"Holy shit!" I said, "Where did all these people come from?" The funny thing was there were only about thirty-five youngsters shouting, "Clean up the Bay! Clean the birds! Clean Standard Oil out!" Demonstrations were right up my alley. I learned long ago that if there was no madness, there was no money. It had been my experience that if one arrived in the midst of confusion, he could usually get what he wanted.

I needed to get through those kids quickly and walk however many feet or miles out onto the wharf, before it was too late. Besides, by that time I was too damn fatigued to cross the street. I leaned hard on my instincts.

A Standard Oil tanker truck loomed in front of me and was slowing down near a gate with a big sign that read "No Private Vehicles." Planning to sneak in behind it, I almost drove off the road following him when he abruptly pulled off the road just short of the gate. I leaned back in the seat, stuck out my chest, looked straight ahead and cruised slowly through.

When the trucks started moving forward, I started with them. My mind was racing with numerous thoughts. *"What the fuck did I come here for? I'll bet that Chet is laughing his ass off."* I was talking to myself. The trucks stopped in front of me. The two in front proceeded past the gate.

I was thinking, *"What am I going to tell these crazy police? Don't tell them shit. Just follow the truck like you work here. See what they say first, then react. White people like to see black people dance. Jump out and start tap dancing. Just be cool and you can handle it."* I hated losers and if I didn't get to the Long Wharf, I was a loser. My whole week would be fucked up and if Chet found out that I came there and did not get in, he would tell every trucker in town. I realized that it was too late to turn around. I had to talk

14

to those police officers and explain why I was behind those trucks, so I got ready for action. The trucks started to roll forward. I looked straight ahead because I was on center stage.

As I inched forward, I thought to myself, *"What am I going to tell these guards?"* All of a sudden, an alarm in my head went off saying, *"Well, if you are going to think of something to say, you better do it now because you are next."*

As the truck in front of me started to pull its load, black smoke billowed out of the twin exhaust pipes that struck upwards. As the trailer began to move, I was sitting still and the person in the Standard Oil pickup truck behind me blew his horn. I touched the gas pedal and my car started to trail the big tanker. As I passed the sentries, I did not stop. I just kept rolling through as if I was in a daze. I rolled about thirty or forty feet before they seemed to realize I was not going to stop.

My determination to drive through was funny because I didn't know where I was going; I had never been on the complex before. However, no one could tell.   For some strange reason, I felt I knew where I was going as if I had been there before. In reality I knew I had never been near there previously. All my life, as far back as I could remember I have always had the feeling of seeing things or being places that I had never seen or been to before. I always thought it was strange.

While I was still in motion, a couple of sleepy guards, not expecting such audacity, were bullshitting near the gate. One of them blew his silly-ass whistle and started running after me shouting, "Hold it!" I knew it was time to stop. He was the regular gate guard; but I observed a lieutenant had been added because of the picketing and possibility of sabotage.

I stopped. The car window was down by the time he jogged up to me. I put the Cad in neutral and turned in the seat so I could size him up. He leaned on the door like he was hot shit and with a redneck southern drawl growled, almost out of wind, "Where in the hell are you going? Where the fuck you think you're going, boy?"

Without giving me time to answer, he unloaded on me about how I was in the wrong place, no one was allowed in and all that shit. So, while his mouth was running and his bad breath was ruining the interior, I reached in the glove compartment, pulled out a writing tablet and then a pen from my shirt pocket. I leaned slowly back in the seat and took a deep breath as he finished saying, "Couldn't you see that sign, boy?" I growled as loud as I could, "What's your name officer?" His mouth dropped open and he looked at me oddly while weakly asking, "What..." I continued to growl, "What's your fuckin' name and badge number?" Poising to write, I held up my pad. "What do you mean?" he asked.

I looked as pissed off as I could and spoke every word very sharply, "Look, I'm from Standard Oil's main office in Los Angeles and I'm the Superintendent in charge of all oil spills in the United States. Now, I've been sent up here to take charge of cleaning up this oil spill and I haven't got time for this shit. Now damn it, what's your fuckin' name and badge number?"

I still held up the pad. He turned a little pasty as he said, "Uh, well uh," and waved frantically for the lieutenant to come over. "Now, since you won't let me in, I'll go back to L.A., but you won't be working here by the time I get to the airport." As the lieutenant got closer, he said, "Uh, wait just a minute," then left to meet him. I watched through the rearview mirror as they met at the back of the car. I clenched my teeth and tightened my stomach to keep from laughing aloud. The redneck was waving his arms and jabbering his ass off while the lieutenant's mouth kept getting wider and wider until a truck could drive through it. I used the time to scratch out a note on the pad. After two or three minutes, they came up to the door with the lieutenant in the lead, leaned on it like Mutt and Jeff and peered in at me. The redneck, leaning awkwardly because the lieutenant was hogging most of the window space, tried to act casual. Clearing his throat so he could mimic an official and important voice, the lieutenant asked, "What's goin' on here?"

By this time, due to being extremely exhausted, I was pissed. Pissed that I might be too late. Pissed that I had to play this game with two low-salaried idiots that could stop me from winning and getting what was rightfully mine if I won.

Therefore, I continued to growl, "Look, I've been sent to take charge of this oil spill." I waved my hand toward the direction of the water. "And I'm late for a meeting right now. So I want you to sign this statement here that you would not let me in this gate." I stuck the pad under the lieutenant's nose.

"Who said we wouldn't let you in?" he asked stupidly, shifting his weight away from the car. "He did," I answered, pointing my pen accusingly at the redneck. He lamely tried to duck and look innocent at the same time. "Hey, I'm real sorry about the mix-up," said the lieutenant as he started filling out a pass. "What's your name?"

"Charlie Walker. But I really think I need to report how you're handling things out here. I especially don't like that damn redneck callin' me 'boy,'" I said, pointing my pen at the redneck again. While looking sheepish, he tried to ease out of my withering stare. "Well, I - I truly am sorry sir. But - but, the best I can do, sir, is to give you your pass," he stammered, as he pressed it gently on my lapel.

Then, as I put the Cad in gear and punched the accelerator, I said, "All right." As I approached the Long Wharf itself, there was another gate. However, the guard had been informed that I was coming, so he opened the gate, smiled and said, "The white building on the right, Mr. Walker. All the contractors are in the main conference room on the second floor. The Chief's office is on the same floor."

I glanced at him, waved my hand and said, "Thank you very much." He said, "I am awfully sorry about that incident. I can assure you it won't happen again." "That's okay."

I did not see another private car anywhere on the pier. I pulled alongside the building, got out very quickly, opened the front

17

door and walked straight up the stairs as if I knew where I was going. Unexplainably, I had the strangest feeling - the feeling that I had been there before. The feeling kind of scared me because of its intensity and its inexplicable origin. Fortunately, it shortly left me and I was soon standing in front of a door with a "Conference Room" sign on it. I opened the door.

Sure enough, the room was packed with people. *"Shit!"* I said to myself. It was full of smoke, contractors and small talk. I knew many of them from previous jobs and socializing, but some were from out of the area. I instantly got the feeling that I was at some kind of auction. I was also beginning to get tired! I shook a couple of hands, said hello and waved at others across the room. As I looked around the room, I could see no other black person. It was easy to flex. When I stepped into a room filled with white men, all of them would turn around and look at me. There was no need for me to look - I was the only black there.

Just as I got that feeling, a small white contractor saw me. "Well, how is the TV star doing?" I looked surprised as I said, "Hello, Ted." "How in the hell are you?" he asked. "What brings you to this neck of the woods?"

Grabbing an empty folding chair, I eased my tired butt into it and looked around - shaking off the exhaustion and revving up my instincts. In the front of the room, three identical executive types in dark colored suits were seated close to each other, muttering back and forth and pausing to bark instructions into a beige colored phone.

A contractor, forty pounds overweight and dressed in khakis and dirtcolored hi-top work shoes, hunched on a chair in front of one of the executives while signing a contract and receiving instructions. In about six minutes, the contractor headed for the door, eyeing the treasure of papers in his hand.

I noticed that though there were several seats in the room, everyone was standing. At that moment, the phone rang and everyone quieted down. A tall, handsome white man answered saying,

"Long Wharf. Yes, yes." He began to write while saying, "Just a moment. Pick up the other phone, Joe!"

Now both of them were writing and saying, "Yeah, yeah." That continued for ten minutes, ending when they finally hung up the phones. The tall, black-haired guy had the best tan I had ever seen; he looked like he had been in a toaster. He said, "Listen up." It got so quiet that I could hear everyone softly breathing and straining to hear his next words.

He continued, "Now look fellows, we are going to need everyone we can muster. We have small areas and lots of them. However, it might require some of you to team up, but don't worry about your money. Each contractor will be given a purchase order with an open end. However, at the end of the day, a Standard Oil rep will sign off on your invoice. We would like to have some kind of billing every day, but remember if you have any problems, feel free to call me. Anyone who does not have my card, come up front and get one." The executive wearing a blue suit that had been doing all the talking looked at me like I had just arrived from Mars. I grinned as big as I could.

To myself I thought, *"Yeah, I know what you're thinking you bigoted piece of shit. You're wondering where this nigga came from. Well, go on shithead, get out of this one."*

Three of us walked up front. He introduced himself to each of us. He extended his hand and with a pleasant smile said, "I am Bill Haines."

"I'm Charlie Walker." He said, "Nice to have you." I could see that he was a well-groomed, smooth, first-class gentleman with interesting eyes. I always looked at a person's eyes. They told me everything I wanted to know about another person. I could tell right off the bat that he was front office - despite his good looks and charm, he did not have any real power. Mr. Haines then stood up and said, "Half Moon Bay. Is there anyone in the room who would like to go to the beaches in Half Moon Bay?" Ten hands immediately shot into the air. One of the three executives selected a contractor.

"San Mateo shoreline?" Mr. Haines continued. More hands. He selected three contractors. "Mr. Jacobs will take care of you gentlemen." Then Mr. Haines abruptly said, "Just a minute. I have got to get someone to go to Stinson Beach. I have been trying since 3 a.m.. Now I must get someone to go take a small amount of equipment and help our people."

No one spoke up and an uneasy silence filled the room. Having just arrived, I still wasn't fully oriented and had no idea what might be left. It didn't register that no one was jumping for it. My instincts said that this was my chance. I ignored everything else.

The silence lasted a few seconds. Taking a deep breath and putting on a smile, I shot my long arm into the air with a wave while saying, "Hey, why don't you integrate and give me the job?" No one said anything. I waved my hand again and said, "Why not?" That time, everyone applauded. Mr. Haines said, "Step right here. I'll take care of you myself." I felt honored. He sat down at the small desk. "Mr. Jacobs," he said, "pass me a purchase order." Mr. Haines said, "Mr. Walker, right?"

"Yes." "Well," he said before pausing to look for a checkmate, "it'll take fifty trucks. You got that many?" I didn't know if he was bluffing and didn't care, but he thought he had me. I thought about how tired and beat up my six dump trucks were. Without blinking I said, "That means three of 'em won't be working." At the same time, I wanted to sign the contract. I couldn't afford any more questions. "Hey, Charlie, that's all right," and "Great Charlie, glad to hear it," came from different places in the room. I didn't drop my focus to see who was talking. More than one knew I was bullshitting, but they weren't giving away the nigga.

Mr. Haines glanced around the room. No one objected. With an imperceptible shrug he reached for a contract. It appeared he should have been more concerned than he was.

Signing the contract was uneventful. He then filled out

another simple-looking form and handed both to me. I couldn't believe my eyes. They seemed to tingle in my hand. He pushed back his chair, stood and dramatically pointed to the paper.

"With this blank purchase order, you can order anything you need to get the job done. We aren't concerned about cost. Just get that damn oil off the beach." He sounded like a pep coach.

He continued, "This is what I need: a couple of blades, about twenty or thirty trucks and four rubber-tired loaders. If they need anything else after you get there, I want you to supply it. That is why I am leaving this purchase order open on one end."

"Thank you, Mr. Haines," I said as I picked up the purchase order. I turned around and several white guys said, "Lots of luck." "Thank you, I am sure I will need it."

At that moment, six white men turned and looked in my mouth, suddenly surprised at the reality of a black man having a contract despite their applause a few seconds earlier. Luckily, I was quick-witted.

I put on a big smile, bugged my eyes and said, "Everyone should own or have a nigga around."

I didn't realize everyone in the room was listening until everyone let out a big laugh.

It seemed to disarm them and make them think, "Oh, he's all right." I was on air as I walked out the door I had just walked in a few moments ago. I had not been there fifteen minutes and I already had my own job; the first real job I had ever gotten on my own, all by myself. I was the boss! Man, to make it in this country, one either had to stay up late or get up early. Before I knew it, I was passing through the very gate that had caused me so much anxiety earlier that morning. More people were standing around.

As I pulled up to leave, the same redneck that called me "boy" saluted and waved me on. I smiled and returned his salute.

I had heard of Stinson Beach, but that was all. It was no one's favorite because the road was a long, narrow, steep grade with hairpin turns. Equipment could easily be lost and at the least, the special maneuvering necessary to get in the big pieces would be very time consuming.

Fortunately, Standard Oil wasn't concerned about the cost, then anyway. The remaining forty-seven trucks I didn't have didn't worry me. I knew if I cut Chet in for fifty percent, he would provide everything I needed and as a fellow white man could pacify the white boys that wouldn't like my tan too well. What I didn't know was the good and bad fortune that signing that contract would eventually dump on me.

# History 3

# "Where is Stinson Beach"

It was hard to believe I was in the game. *"By the way,"* I said to myself, *"where the fuck is Stinson Beach?"* Well, I figured it must be near San Francisco, so I started toward the San Francisco Bay Bridge. I later learned that Chet and several white truckers were standing around having a field day laughing about my supposed wild goose chase because everyone thought it was impossible to get into the Standard Oil Reservation.

Guessing at where Stinson Beach was, I drove toward the Bay Bridge. In about twenty-five minutes I reached the toll plaza leaving Emeryville and decided it was time to ask for better directions. As I approached the Bridge, a highway patrolman in shiny black boots with tight pants shoved up his crack was giving a guy a ticket. I pulled over.

"Um, excuse me officer, do you know where Stinson Beach is?" "Where did you just come from?" "Richmond." "You were right there. Just across the San Rafael Bridge and left on 101." "Shit!"

I found out that I was near it when I was at the Standard Oil Refinery. I was actually going away from it. Well, I got on the right track. I turned around and went back to the San Rafael Bridge.

Around 9:30 a.m., near Mill Valley, I saw the sign leading

23

toward Stinson Beach and turned off Highway 101. A mountain ridge loomed in front of me and I knew my destination was on the other side of it.

I should have gotten a ticket because I drove at eighty-five miles per hour all the way, at least until I started up the grade. By this time, my ass was really dragging. I let down the windows. I thought this was no place to be nodding. I could not believe the roads; they had curves that were complete turnarounds. I also met a pickup head-on. I could never figure out how he missed hitting me. That incident frightened me to complete awareness. I continued to drive along the winding road.

I went down one hill, then up another, followed by curve after curve. Out of nowhere I hit a steep incline and continued up, up, up. I relaxed only to hit another steep curve. As I came out of the last curve, a complete view of the world seemed to unfold. The view was beautiful and awesome! I saw the sun-kissed horizon that seemed to embody the limitless possibilities open to me as I headed toward the biggest job of my life. Birds flew in a gentle rhythm as they glided on the air.

I felt like a baby bird that had just learned how to use his wings and had discovered a new world. Everyone in the world should have seen that view, which clearly demonstrated Mother Nature's artistic ability that no man could duplicate. As much of a rush as I was in, I had to stop and look. I said, "Beauty is not in the eye of the beholder. This is beautiful in everyone's eyes!"

I got back in the Cad and drove to the job site. As I looked over the valley, I could see everything including the job site; it was no problem to find.

The calm breeze from earlier in the morning was now bending the grass and brushing against the trees. Some people walking near the road were leaning slightly into the wind. It felt good to be in a comfortable car traveling toward challenging business - even if there was a suspicion in the back of my mind that this was a tougher situation than I really wanted.

Monotonous curves and unusually heavy traffic soon slowed my progress. Then, halfway up the mountain, traffic slowed to a crawl. I was part of a long line of cars, trucks and motorcycles of every size and shape going in my direction.

Topping the summit, I was greeted with a magnificent expanse of endless blue ocean like the endless opportunities available to one who would make the effort to go after them. Nestled at the base of the mountain, with a glistening ribbon of sand separated in front of the breaking waves, was the little hamlet of Stinson Beach. It was possessed by the wealthy, but many San Franciscans considered it their favorite respite from civilized pressures.

Out on the water, like a huge blight, a wide expanse of oil wiggled gently with the pulse of the water. Smaller blobs were spreading out from it - the foremost pieces struggling with the breaking waves. Some of the oil had already violated the beach and was increasingly contaminating the worshiped sand. To those trying to pass me in their rush to the beach, it was dismay; to me, it was money in the rough.

The winding road narrowed on the descent and became unbelievably steep - some of the curves were double hairpin turns. I wondered how in the hell we'd ever get heavy equipment through there and was beginning to understand why none of the other contractors wanted the job.

Finally, the road unwound and as it leveled, it swung out and along the beach. Neatly painted forty-year-old clapboard cottages and shops squatted on the mountainside of the road - each one peering at the sapphire blue water. Tucked near the road along the ocean-side, was a two-story motel, several old cabin-sized buildings, a Ranger Station, and at the far end a small restaurant.

Shade trees dotted around and between the buildings. The

heavy wind was almost imperceptible in this protected cup in the mountain. I was told later that the wind always swept up off the water, over the beach and onto the top of the mountain - similar to trying to force air into a bottle. This, of course, made Stinson Beach very pleasant even while everywhere else was cold and windy.

Like lemmings on the move, people jostled their way toward the beach. All of them stared at the growing ugliness that contaminated their precious playground. Several dune buggies and four-wheel-drive vehicles were chasing each other up and down the beach next to the surf, flinging globs of black jelly in every direction as they went. For some glorious reason, some of the people had to go out and personally experience the globs of crude oil. Some of them were tracking it back up from the beach - shaking and stomping their feet and looking down in dumbfounded dismay.

The four-wheelers had been at it a while because the main road and the side streets that cut between the cottages and disappeared back toward the hidden custom homes were smeared with trails of oil and splattered little globs that looked like they were melting into the street. In forays of foolishness and ignorance, the lemmings had further tracked it in every direction, including into the shops.

The day was unusually warm, even for Stinson Beach, but especially for January. Scantily clad women milling about seemed to add a festive mood; it made me feel festive anyway. Several young guys were unloading a truck and trailer load of hay. I wondered if they were going to have a pony ride at the circus, but I didn't see a herd of horses anywhere. The people looked comical enough, although I did not have time to grow curious.

I picked a spot near the road close to the Ranger Station and parked directly under a huge tree to shade my Cad. The gritty sound of sand crunching under my feet announced my arrival to no one in particular.

The heavy smell of hay challenged by the salty air didn't mix well in my nose. As I neared the Ranger Station, I realized that many in the crowd seemed to be watching some kind of activity. I also looked in that same direction, down by the sea where the black blob grew. I could see a parade of "yes men" in business suits sauntering back and forth with great importance. Hovering over them and stumbling back and forth at the same tempo was a crowd of cameramen and news reporters trying to catch every vain word and meaningless promise.

After staring at the show for a while, I climbed the four steps leading into the Ranger Station. I was reminded again that my strength was tapped out from no sleep. Turning the knob, I leaned into the door and pushed it open, took three or four steps to a wooden customer counter and peered at the half-dozen office types doing office-related activities.

The closest underling noticed me clearing my throat, saw that I was black and went back to being very busy. This had happened so many times in my life that it was hard to even bother getting irritated. I stood there a moment or two looking around the office and checked out the action. A little honey in tight pants and a frilly blouse was on the phone "yes sir-ing" some bastard.

I listened closely to hear her say, "Yes sir, we've ordered the hay. One load has arrived and they're unloading it. The other nine are to arrive shortly."

Pause.

"Yes sir. Mr. Shard is handling that sir. We're recruiting more volunteers to help all the time."

Pause.

"Yes sir. I'll tell him."

*"So they ordered that damned hay,"* I thought, *"and they're going to make a bigger mess. Good. They'll pay me more to clean it up."*

Tuning out the chick, I stared at the underling who was ignoring me and without giving it a lot of consideration, took a deep breath and whistled very loudly through my teeth. Now I was on stage. I ignored the shocked looks around the room and pointed my finger at the asshole now looking at me with a "What do you want, nigger?" look. I only half-heartedly tried to smile and motioned with my finger for him to come to me.

He stood, headed toward me and intoned a little too high and sweetly to be sincere, "May I help you?"

"Two hamburgers and a milkshake," rumbled over my lips before I could squash the urge. Putting on a bigger smile to outdo his banal one, I jerked my thumb toward the beach and said patiently, "I'm the contractor who's going to clean up that mess."

"Oh." Pressing my hands firmly into the counter to keep from grabbing his scrawny neck, I dropped my smile into my best deadpan hard stare and slowly and deliberately reached inside my coat and pulled out the blank purchase order. While extending it toward him, my unblinking stare made him fidget.

He appeared to be about twenty-five years old, stupid, maybe a faggot and definitely underpaid. He eased the last few feet between us, accepted the piece of paper and stood stiffly reading it for a moment. Finally he realized what he was holding and his face lit up and flushed.

"Oh, you're here!" he cooed. He pivoted to move around the counter and I reached and grabbed the purchase order as he moved away. As he dashed out the door I could hear him yell, "Hey, Mr. Shard, the contractor is here!"

The next yell was further away, so I knew he was going out to meet this Mr. Shard.

"Warn him I'm a nigga," I sighed as I slumped into an arm-chair, closed my eyes and dozed off.

The entire parade of executives and reporters hustled across

28

the loose sand and twenty-five of them must have entered the door at the same time. Initially, I was aware of what appeared to be a roar from the scuffling feet combined with extensive panting from the effort of twenty-five sets of heaving lungs. My head was slumped on my chest and I opened my eyes without moving. Oil was smeared and dripping all over the floor, mixed with crunching black sand. Every pair of trousers was drenched with oil and sand up to the knees. As I looked higher, I saw three camera lenses and several microphones pointed at me. On impulse, I reached in my coat for my piece. I then realized I wasn't carrying it and at the same time woke up enough to know it wasn't necessary.

A hand was stuck out a couple of feet from me that belonged to a suave white man who was cleanshaven with graying hair and a psychiatrist's smile. He was impeccably dressed in a medium gray three-piece suit with oil running down his trousers and shoes. He looked like the leader of the gang.

"Sure glad you're here," he declared. "I'm Wesley Shard, Vice President of Standard Oil's San Francisco office."

He didn't indicate that he could see I was the only black within miles, but we both knew and understood as we looked into each other's eyes.

Reaching for his hand and pushing myself slowly up out of the chair, I concentrated on clearing my head and waking up my body.

"Charlie Walker, owner of Walker Trucking," I said carefully.

"Glad to meet you," he replied. Like chickens pecking at one ear of corn, a dozen press voices exploded:

"Mr. Walker, how are you going to handle this?"

"Mr. Walker, have you done this kind of thing before?"

"Mr. Walker, how soon can you start cleaning up the oil?"

"Mr. Walker, what kind of equipment do you have?"

"Mr. Walker, blah, blah, blah...?"

"Mr. Walker, blah, blah, blah...?"

Immediately, electricity and power surged through my body. Taking a deep breath while slowly looking around the room, I let the feeling of prestige soak in and felt the heightening alertness flow through me. The press was something I knew how to handle. I knew how to give them what they wanted and not tell them what they didn't need to know.

Then, looking very calm and relaxed with my nose in the air, I measured my words carefully.

"I'm going to do whatever it takes to get every bit of oil off this beautiful beach and out of every ravine and inlet. In fact, this place will be in better condition when I leave it than it's ever been before. Standard Oil is very concerned about the environment and wants to do everything it can to correct this unfortunate accident. Consequently, I have been given the authority, at any cost, to get this mess hauled away. Every resource that is needed is available to me. I will use the best equipment and the most experienced personnel to do the job as quickly as is humanly possible."

They all smiled and nodded their heads while some furiously took notes. As I took a breath, Mr. Shard jumped in and said, "I'm sure that Mr. Walker and Standard Oil will work very well together. This man was the best expert we could find on the West Coast to take over this operation. We are very impressed with his credentials and consider ourselves very lucky to have him on such short notice." He lied so fucking well that I almost laughed. I could see that he was proud of me too.

"Mr. Walker, Mr. Walker, blah, blah, blah...?" went a dozen voices. Holding my hands up and shaking my head, I said, "People, the operation must come first. We have no time to lose. I need to get out there immediately to look at what I'm up against." Touching my arm lightly and turning as he spoke, Mr. Shard said, "Right this way, Mr. Walker," and started out the door.

Our entourage followed right on our heels, yammering as we went. I kept a fast pace next to Shard. The reporters turned on the other executives trailing behind us.

At the edge of the expansive mass, Shard just started slopping through it. I put on the brakes. I was not about to ruin my expensive suit. Everyone piled up behind me like dominoes. Shard walked on for a few yards jabbering away.

"Now you can see most of the oil is just sitting on top of the sand and shouldn't be too tough to handle. But a hell of a problem is getting the oil out of those ravines," he said sweeping his arms and pointing as he went.

Finally, he realized he was the only one slogging through the oil and waved his arm for me to come join him. "Oh, to hell with the oil, Charlie. We'll buy you a new suit." I shrugged and strode forward. "What the hell?" I muttered. "I might even be able to squeeze two suits out of this dude."

We started up the beach away from most of the activity. As I slowly began picking my way through the squishing jelly, I noticed how dismally alive it was. Several sea lions, scores of seagulls, snappers and ducks, all completely blackened, floundered hopelessly about in the last throes of life. Flopping fish accented the dismay further. The breaking waves, normally foamy white, were now foamy black. Each incoming wave left behind huge clumps of oil and each new wave left more than the last. The ocean looked like a giant monster trying to spit out something that tasted awful. The main oil slick edged near the beach and within hours would all be dumped in the surrounding few miles.

Noticing me stopping to stare out at the slick, Shard stepped closer to me so the press couldn't hear him.

"You're going to make out on this a lot better than you might have thought, Charlie. I talked to the guys down on the wharf earlier. We initially thought this area was going to be fairly light. We expected most of it to end up around Half Moon Bay. However, the wind came up, changed direction and starting around 7:00 this morning, as you can see, most of the oil started being dumped right

31

in this area. That's why all the emergency crews are concentrated at San Francisco Beach and in the San Francisco area."

I smiled wryly and said, "Things do have a way of turning around, don't they?" To keep the press from having too much of a chance to interrupt, I tried to stay totally occupied with Shard. We walked a little further to the northern end of the sand and watched as the oil surged and splashed against the rocky cliff with each wave. Where the sand ended, the land jutted out into the water at a ninety-degree angle and rose steeply into a high, magnificent, rocky hill, covered with scrub and evergreen-like trees.

While pointing at the jutting land, Shard said, "That's a natural breakwater and around behind it, there is a nice quiet, well-protected, little cove with all sorts of boats in it. That oil is creeping in there like it's attracted by strange forces. We're going to catch hell cleaning those boats, not to mention the work it will take to get all the oil out of there."

We stood looking at the mess for a while like two little boys that had just broken their favorite toy. In the inlets and ravines that I could see, the oil was so pitch black and thick that it looked like it was growing there.

Still staring, I said, "Yeah, but that's nothing compared to the difficulty of getting the oil off those rocks and out of the ravines and shit." I continued to stare at the new patches of oil colliding into the rocks. Thoughts ran through my mind of various ways of getting it out. After a while Shard began to fidget because I still hadn't moved a muscle. Finally, I looked at Shard and smiled.

"Wesley, you're right. It'll have to be taken out by hand, but with a couple of choppers with fifty-gallon drums hanging from them; we can lower the workers down and drop them off. When they have scooped up enough to fill the barrels, the choppers can bring in empty ones and pick up the full ones." Shard looked at me with his mouth open, then turned his head toward the water for an instant and looked back at me like a delighted kid.

32

"Hot damn! That'll work Charlie! I'll get those choppers sent out here as soon as we get back." We stood there a moment longer. Then Shard reached over and pulled me a little closer to the edge of the beach so the noise of the surf pounding against the rocks was louder and no one could hear us.

He whispered, "Now Charlie, you can see what a bitch of a mess this is. You know how damaging the press can be. We've got to look like we're bustin' our asses. I don't give a damn what it costs, get as much equipment up here as you can. It doesn't matter what it is or even if it runs. Just load this damn town with enough machinery to sink it. Do I have anything to worry about?"

"I am the best that ever done it." He chuckled. I went on, "No problem. Wesley, as soon as I get back to the Ranger Station, I'll make the necessary calls." I smelled a suitcase full of money. Shard said, "By the way, you can stay at the Seadrift Motel. You are going to be so busy that you won't have time to go home. I already rented the entire motel for all Standard Oil employees." I replied, "That's fine as long as I can have two rooms." Shard asked, "Why?"

I nonchalantly answered, "I need one for me and one for my girls." Shard eyed me suspiciously and said, "You old dog." I replied, "Yeah, my daughters are messy and they aren't messing up my room!" I showed him their most recent school portraits and we both laughed over the matter. We turned around and headed in the direction of the Ranger Station while looking down at the entire beach. The playground of sand was about five or six blocks long. Beyond that, the cliffs with their inlets and ravines began again. The slimy oil was piling higher and thicker on the beach while the number of vehicles cavorting up and down the beach increased. I couldn't understand how the hell anyone thought it was fun to be covered with slime that would be so damn hard to remove.

As we sauntered back, walking in the loose sand to keep

33

from being run over by the vehicles flying through the hard sand next to the breaking waves, I could see that all ten loads of hay had arrived and that most of it had been unloaded. Several hundred volunteers from the town and wherever the hell the rest of them came from were furiously spreading the hay.

Now where there had been oil on the streets, there was straw-oil. I knew that damn straw wouldn't soak up one molecule of oil, but would just smear it further. The town looked like it had been tarred and strawed.

A few dozen bales were put on pickup trucks and hauled to strategic spots in the town and along the beach. Some of the hay was spread on the oil lying on the beach and a good share sloshed around in the surf. Bales were stacked up and the outer ones were broken open. Teenagers were using the bales to have hilarious hay fights.

A flatbed truck stacked high with hay was making its way up one of the streets leading to a home behind the hamlet. The driver obviously wasn't going to unload it until he got to his barn.

We walked a few yards further and were in the midst of "Happy Hay Land." However, I still needed to get to a phone. The press had broken up and wandered off in different directions, some to their cars. After checking out the action, I turned to Shard with my hands in my pockets and asked as nonchalantly as I could, "Who came up with the idea of bringing in all this hay?"

Shard turned to the trailing executives and pointed at a short chubby one.

"Milton there came up with the idea, didn't you Milton?"
"Oh yes, I did," he chirped, gleeful to be in on the big boy's conversation. Oozing with enthusiasm, he continued.

"The townspeople have been very helpful. I met with a group of concerned citizens early this morning to answer their questions about our progress. One of them said that their grandmother used

34

straw to clean grease, so it should work well in soaking up the oil. Everyone there agreed that it was a grand idea. So what more could I do?" Smiling and bouncing along beside us, he looked like a happy little cherub that just discovered the recipe to cure the world's problems. Then he edged even closer to us and spoke in a really low voice saying, "And, you know, it's very important to keep the townspeople happy. They could be very nasty if they got mad. And look how they have been helping us."

He majestically swept his arms out toward the anthill of people throwing hay. "Yes indeed, Milton. I can sure see what a good idea it was," I answered incredulously. The cash register rang in my mind again.

I was then distracted by half a dozen nearby college-age guys who were sprawled on a huge pile of hay and stoned out of their minds. They were passing around a couple of joints. I watched one of them, a huge oafish looking guy, with a scraggly beard who was wearing rotten jeans and a T-shirt he must have used to wipe the bottom of his car. He was trying to hold a joint to his lips. After several unsuccessful attempts, he finally dropped it between his legs and laughed like a hyena as he watched it smoldering in the hay.

"Come on, Carl. Pass the fuckin' weed," urged another hooligan. Still laughing hysterically, Carl gurgled, "Look at the motherfucker, will ya? The smoke is all green and shit."

Then he started piling more hay on top of it and blew on it while making loud noises. "Hey, look at that fuckin' Carl," another one yelled as he began to giggle. "He's gonna roast his fuckin' nuts!" The rest of them raised themselves in enough time to see the flames rise between the fool's legs. All of them burst into raucous laughter. One rolled onto the sand cackling so hard I thought he was going to swallow his tongue.

Carl never moved. He belly bounced up and down as he laughed like a lunatic.

"Is this really happening?" asked Shard. "If I didn't see it, I wouldn't believe it!" I'd have let the pig roast, but some of the press people were only yards away and I could just see the hell the fire department and every government agency in the country would give us. Besides, I had a profit to protect. So I ran the few feet to the pile of hay, grabbed Carl's greasy jeans and dragged him right with the fire. He was sitting close enough to the edge of the pile that most of the burning straw came with him. Then grabbing a limp arm, I pulled him - still cackling - away before he could get burned. Then with my feet, I scattered the hay and stomped it into the sand. Looking around, I saw a few people watching, but we weren't a major attraction yet. Then looking over the rest of the scruffy bunch, I instinctively picked out the leader and walked over to him. "Hey man, why don't you and your partners move on?"

# History 4

# "In Stinson Beach City"

As I walked up old 101 North, through the little quaint town, the trees leaned over one side of the highway and gently touched the other side as if in tender embrace. As the trees kissed each other, a beam of sunlight penetrated the dense foliage, causing the light to reflect in a million places. I sensed the wind humming a sweet melody that the trees, flowers, butterflies, animals and everything alive danced to and used as its bodily rhythm. My mind was having an orgasm. That's the feeling I got when nothing could go wrong.

Stinson Beach was a wonderful place. I continually tried to figure out how Alfred Hitchcock missed making one of his horror pictures there.

As I approached my office, at least the little shack they had given me, Mr. Shard looked out the door and said, "We are waiting for you, Mr. Walker."

"Yes, can I help you, Mr. Shard?"

"Yes, Mr. Walker. Mr. Tennat is in the office and would like to meet with you."

I replied, "Sorry if I kept everyone waiting." I thought to myself, *"This asshole can be a real ass. He looks like the cat that ate the canary."*

I stepped through the door with an air of importance as I whispered to Mr. Shard, "Who the fuck is Mr. Tennat?"

He whispered back, "Everybody's boss."

"Just the man I am looking for."

Mr. Shard turned quickly and we both stepped into a room on the right side of the hallway, which contained a card table with five or six glasses surrounding a small pitcher of water. I got a strange feeling as Mr. Tennat looked up and Mr. Shard said, "This is Mr. Walker, our contractor."

Mr. Tennat seemed a little shocked as if he wanted to say, "These assholes did not tell me he's a nigger, oh, I mean black." I was a salesman and could read expressions. I smiled back at him as if to say, "Yes, it's me and now that we have integrated, you are going to be seeing lots of us everywhere."

I sat down. He didn't attempt to stand and shake my hand and I never shook hands with people when they were sitting, man or woman, unless they were in a wheel chair. I did not notice when I entered that there were two other men sitting in the far right corner. However, I saw them out of the corner of my eye, but did not turn around to stare at them.

Tennat cleared his throat and said, "Listen carefully, Walker. You are on our team and you are a leader. We trust all our leaders to look out for Standard Oil. Don't talk to anyone from the press. You run the job. We are the largest corporation in the world. When a leader speaks, he gets respect, but he also knows how to give orders. Most of all, he knows how to follow orders."

He looked over to his left and said, "Bob, I'll be ready to leave in ten minutes."

From what he said, I knew he and Shard had been talking about me. However, Shard kept it to himself that I was black, which was his way of making a joke.

Tennat started to chitchat, trying to find out how much I knew about the trade, all the while sizing me up. I thought he didn't like what

38

he saw. All of a sudden, I heard a loud noise. My mind raced as the sound came through; it eventually registered as a helicopter. I had not heard it when it arrived. I said without thinking, "I sure could use one of those." Tennat asked, "One of what?"

"One helicopter at least. I could lower men down in those ravines and scoop out all that oil. That's the only safe way to do it, I think."

His whole face lit up. "That's what I like, a man of action." I smiled as he said, "I'll send you two, one for work and one for your personal use."

That was his way of showing Shard that he also made jokes. "You should have them within the hour. This way you can survey all the damage and give me a full report."

The helicopter was truly an off-the-cuff thought. I didn't think he would agree so readily. Both white men stood up and filed past my back. Tennat left at a fast pace with Shard tagging along behind him. They were running as I saw them pass the window. Tennat stopped short of the helicopter and Shard walked right up to his back.

Tennat turned and said a few things to Shard. It appeared from the window that Tennat told Shard to take his ass back to work because when Shard returned, I could see that he did not like what the boss had said. I wanted to laugh in his face because no one liked to be the butt of a joke.

Shard started babbling, "Chuck, Mr. Tennat said he will be back later. Put Walker over everything and everybody. He is in charge." I wanted to flex, but I remained nonchalant.

"Also, tell Dan Wakeman of Industrial Railway that he will handle all payrolls on his force account and give Walker whatever he wants. Let's get this job rolling. Walker knows what he wants. I'll talk to you later. Call me until you catch me. By the way, I am sending Walker two choppers. He knows what to use them for."

Shard spouted all that in one burst. Tennat ran, jumping into his chopper and lifted right off. I later learned that when he got in the helicopter, he told the pilot, "Shard didn't tell me the contractor was black, so I put him over everybody. See how he likes that. I am sure it is not so funny now."

Later, that day I went over to the Standard Oil main office and ran into Tennat's helicopter pilot. We both had a big laugh about it. Tennat also laughed during the entire helicopter ride back to his office.

I looked at Shard and said, "I thought he didn't like me."

Shard replied, "He respects you. I have never in fifteen years seen him just turn a new man loose the way he did you."

With that remark, Shard looked me in the eyes and said, "I'm with you, boss. What do you want me to do?"

I thought, *"I don't want you to forget I am in charge, but most of all stop making jokes."* I didn't say those things, but I felt compelled to issue at least one order.

I replied, "Get Chet Smith on the phone. He is a contractor in San Francisco. I am going to need him. Also, who is Dan Wakeman?" Shard answered, "Dan Wakeman is a top executive for Industrial Railway, which handles the force accounts for any emergencies that come up and I would call this an emergency. They're not on the in-house staff, but we just call them up when something happens and they come on the scene and help us take care of it." I said, "Well, I know about force accounts. I just wanted to know who is this Dan Wakeman."

Shard replied, "Is that all, boss?" I said, "I am going down to the bar. When my helicopters come, I want you to come and get me. Tell the pilot to stand by and also find out if we can land in Candlestick Park's parking lot. Also tell Chet I'll be there within an hour and a half, if it is okay for us to land."

I couldn't wait to leave and go get a drink. I had a strong urge to have a drink as if I was hooked on booze. As I sat in the bar having three rum and cokes, one right after another, I realized that I had to keep cool, act aloof and keep everyone on his toes. While I sat at the bar, a guy from a trucking company sat next to me and said he wanted to talk to me. However, the last thing I wanted at that moment was to have a conversation. As I was getting ready to tell this guy that I didn't want to talk, I heard a loud propeller noise. It was the sound of helicopters. I got up and went outside. As I looked in the direction of the sound, I saw three helicopters landing. It was around dusk and the spotlights were on while their nightlights were flashing. The light from the helicopters lit up the area brighter than daylight.

I walked back down the two blocks I had just walked up before I met Mr. Tennat. My life seemed to be a movie. I kept thinking, *"This can't be real. How did I do all this?"* But I put those thoughts in the back of my mind, and responded to the moment at hand.

At that instant all hell broke loose. Some teenagers had beaten a Standard Oil supervisor because he had made a smart remark! I found out about five minutes later that he called one of those boys who were smoking weed earlier a doper. When I saw him, it was clear that they had beaten his ass. I wanted to laugh when I saw him on the stretcher. Both of his eyes were black around the outer sides up to his eyebrows. He looked like a raccoon and all his clothes had been torn up and hanging off him. I said, to myself, *"This mother-fucka looks like he was in a hatchet fight and everyone had a hatchet but him."*

I walked into the office to get myself together and noticed that Dan Wakeman had moved into the office because I saw a tall pile of receipts and order forms cluttered on a desk that could only belong to the man handling the money. As I turned around to come out, Dan, Shard and three other Standard Oil employees entered. All of them looked me in the eyes and asked in unison, "What are we gonna do?"

"For one thing, since that guy is in such bad shape, get him to the hospital. Don't wait for an ambulance! Between you and me,

41

he is lucky those kids didn't kill him." I looked over Dan's shoulder and saw the boys who had just beaten up the Standard Oil supervisor. In my mind, I named him, "Raccoon."

I walked past Dan and right up into the largest youngster's face and said, "You beat him up, but I'll beat your ass if any one of you touch me. If you rat-pack me, somebody is going to the morgue. Now what the fuck do you want?"

The one with red hair said, "He shoved Fred first. We were not bothering him. We just wanted to tell his boss that you guys couldn't come out here and push us around."

I said, "You are talking to his boss." The youngster's eyes got big and he looked me up and down. Before he could say anything else, I said, "Look, I am not going to get into a shouting match with you."

As I turned, Dan and everyone else stared at me.

I said, "Look, Dan, why don't you men go next door and leave us to talk for a few minutes." Dan led Shard and three other Standard Oil employees out. About fifteen young guys tried to come in and I said, "Not everybody." I could tell the leaders right away: six guys and a young lady who dressed and acted boyish. She was quite attractive. As soon as the door closed, two guys and the young lady lit up a large joint.

There were only three chairs, so I grabbed one, sat down and said, "Lock the door, please, and pass me a joint."

The girl jumped up and said, "Well all-l-l-l right-t-t." She stuck her hand in her tight pants, pulled out a bag of weed and said, "Let me roll you one." I laughed and said, "That's cool."

All of the youngsters lit up and said, "You are all right. By the way, this is Columbian, the best."

"Let's get this straight. Even though the guy whose ass you kicked had it coming, you didn't have to do that. If anyone says or does anything wrong, you have my permission to tell them I said I will not tolerate bad conduct. We are in your community. What has occurred here is not any of you people's fault.  I understand tension is high, but I will not tolerate bad conduct on our part, or yours.  At best let's make every attempt to work together."

The red-headed kid skeptically asked, "Are you kidding?  You are in charge of all this?"

I said, "You got that right."  The girl handed me the joint she had just rolled and I lit up. We smoked the joint and talked.  All of them asked me a hundred questions.  I could tell they wanted to ask me how I became the boss, but they never mentioned it.  They were very intelligent and I immediately admired them.

I felt their vibes and sensed that they would be pivotal to maintaining peace in the community.  I shared with them the fact that I was an outside contractor and Standard Oil put me in charge of the cleanup because that was my specialty.  They understood right away.  They sensed my vibes and knew that I would do whatever it took to get the job done.

While we were talking, the telephone installer arrived.  He knocked on the door and I shouted, "Go away."

Everyone fell out laughing.  Through those youngsters, all the hippies and militants in the town got to know me.

I had to go to a meeting at the Long Wharf with all of the executives, headed by Stanley Smith, the executive in charge of environmental friendliness, hence the executive's ass that was really on the line.  The purpose of the meeting was to discuss my initial game plan.  I let the youngsters finish the joint while I cleared my head and prepared for the meeting.  I soon told them that I had to leave, but they could visit me anytime to talk and get a little toot.  They said they'd be back soon and quickly filed out of my office.  I sat down for a moment to collect my thoughts.  I really didn't have a game plan and I didn't know what these executives wanted, but I knew that I would somehow give it to them.

I headed for my helicopter, *"My,"* I thought, *"from a paid-off Fleetwood to a helicopter, I'm getting paid to ride in."*  I expectantly entered the conference room full of waiting executives. It turned out to be a good meeting. The Standard Oil officials bragged, "As far as I am concerned, Mr. Walker this, Mr. Walker that."

I learned that the people in the office didn't really know what was going on outside on the beach. I felt Standard Oil subscribed to the old saying, "Don't let your right hand know what your left hand is doing." They lived up to it because their right hand had never even heard of a left hand.

The meeting was over in thirty minutes and in essence I was told, "Spend as much money as you have to and then some. Make everybody happy."

I shook everyone's hand. I gave the businessman's smile, the one that said, "Trust me." All businessmen knew all the smiles. The next smile was the "I got to go" smile. Everyone in the world knew that one; there was nothing to it. It simply said, "Would you shut the fuck up so I can say goodbye!"

I went back to the chopper and arrived at Stinson Beach four minutes later. When I entered the office, I was immediately confronted with community needs. Standard Oil had approved a shipment of butter, a shipment of mineral oil and two hundred tons of hay. Chet, who had arrived when I was gone, stood in amazement.

"Charlie, did you order all this shit?" "What shit? I just came from a meeting at the Long Wharf. Slow down. What is going on?" "Since you left for the meeting, some hippies came up here and said they wanted all these different items and Shard called someone and got their okay. It will arrive tomorrow."

"Chet, that's all right. Whatever the townspeople want, we have been ordered to supply it, right or wrong." As I looked around, everyone was looking in my mouth. "Chet, step over here." As he moved towards me, I looked for a spot to conference with him, and not be overheard. Chet, sensing my mood swing for privacy, followed. I whispered, "Look, Chester, Standard Oil doesn't know what to do. They have never been confronted with anything like this

44

before. The more money they spend, the more money we make because if they spend 5 million dollars, it will all go through our books and I make fifteen percent. If you figure that out, split between you and me, profit and overhead, I will get $375,000 and you will get the same. The big ones baby, more than a quarter of a million dollars apiece."

We shook hands and nodded in agreement. From that point on, it was "high ho, silver." I was amazed at how quickly Chet had equipment arriving. However, no one knew the best way to proceed. As I turned to go over the job, I saw a bunch of youngsters leading a group of people up to the makeshift Standard Oil office, which consisted of only three little bungalows.

I immediately sensed trouble. I stood where I was and waited for them to reach me. I was surprised that there was no shouting and one of the young ladies was crying. They said all the sea animals were dying. "We want one of your people to come look at what you have done."

I said, "Let's go. We are going to straighten it out." I joined the group and proceeded over to the cave and sure enough, the closer I got, the more it began to smell. Apparently, dead mammals began to smell just a few hours after death.

I counted seven dead sea lions; at least that's what I thought they were. There must have been forty or fifty people with me. I turned to the crowd and said, "As you can see, we are moving with the clean up in order to minimize this type of thing. I am going to create a new cleanup crew especially for dead animals. Also, I am going to get someone else over here right away. I want an autopsy performed so we can see what we can do to prevent this from happening again."

I saw they respected and listened to what I was saying. "So watch. I can show you better than I can tell you. I am not some lazy executive. I will do what I say!" Ten days later, Standard Oil held a funeral for all the dead animals. I couldn't plan it because I had too many other things to handle. However, I gave the task to Shard and he produced great results. I had Chet go so he could report back to me on how it turned out and so the community would see that high-level employees were concerned about the animals. Chet later told me that Shard outdid himself because the funeral was just like a typical one held for people. Each animal had its own small wooden coffin.

A minister of some denomination performed the ceremony and wished the animals off to "a world where oil could never touch them again." In total, Standard Oil spent over $15,000, but it was money well spent because the town loved us for it.

After my impromptu speech, I started through the crowd. As I did, the young lady whom I had seen yesterday with the weed grabbed my arm and said, "Let's go smoke a joint."

I said, "Okay, but let me get this assigned to the right people. Tell me where you guys are going to be. Look, let me give you some money. Today the treat is on me." She said, "Far out." I looked up and saw Chet coming in our direction. I ran out to him and said, "I need a couple of hundred bucks." He stuck his hand in his rear pocket and pulled out his wallet. I said, "Just give me three of those bills." He handed me all the money in his wallet. It turned out to be $370. By this time, the young lady had walked up to me.

I said, "You and Paul follow me to my office. By the way, what is your name?"

"Fran."

"Okay Fran. You and Paul go inside with Mr. Smith. I will be right there and bring the money," I whispered as everyone spilled into my office and listened to me give orders. Chet started giving me his report in front of people from the community.

"We are digging into the sand. There is hay everywhere. We now have a work force of over two hundred people plus volunteers."

As I listened to Chet, I observed that Claudia, Chet's daughter, was sitting in the office. I counted five telephone men. The whole town was being strangled with equipment. I could see progress, but the press was keeping a high profile. Chet was saying other things such as, "You have a tour with Industrial Railway and Standard Oil," to the press and various community members.

After I had heard enough, I loudly said, "Look Chet, I am going to go to a town meeting. Would you cancel all meetings for me today until 7:30 this evening? It's all right if you handle these things. We can discuss it at our 9 p.m. meeting. Now ladies and gentlemen, we can move to the real business."

As I said that, the youngsters said, "Right on man!" I lost some of the people from my office with the help of Fran. I looked to the right and saw my car parked and dusty. I then remembered that I had not touched it since I parked it there two days ago. I stopped short and said, "Say you guys, I am going to bring my car. How many of you would like to ride with me?"

Fran said, "Hold it!"

As I unlocked the car, I heard her say, "Mike, Jeff, Al, Pluck, Ted." All of them nearly ran over me while trying to climb into the Cad. I said to myself, *"Umph, I like her take charge attitude."* I could remember looking back, all the way back, to the cotton fields of Mississippi, remembering those strong black females in the cotton field that had that same kind of attitude over those young growing boys, but looking like men, as they ordered them in sternness, but love. I smiled, walked around to the other side and entered from the driver's side. I stuck the key in the ignition, cranked the car, put it in reverse and looked out of the rearview window all in one motion. The radio, air conditioner and lights went on and a bell rang reminding me to fasten my seat belt. Cadillacs were impressive.

One of the fellows in the back seat said, "Let's get a little toot." I said, "Now that's what I am talking about." Everyone in the car said, "Right on, brothers." Fran said, "Let's go to my cousin's house." I pulled over to the side of the road and said, "You guys know where we are going?"

Everyone said, "Let me drive."

I said, "Fran, why don't you drive?"

She said, "I don't have a license."

Al said, "I have my license."

I said, "Okay, it's you."

He got out and sat in the driver's seat while Fran moved to the middle front seat and I sat on the front passenger side. Al said, "I know where everything is." Fran said, "Go up to my cousin's."

Al proceeded carefully. A few blocks later we pulled into a driveway and everyone got out and began walking toward the backyard. A slight breeze circulated that was incredibly fresh and similar to air from the country; I felt extremely free. I then understood why people moved out of the city. *"Awesome,"* I thought, *"such freshness!"*

We passed a swimming pool. The house looked warm and the smell of food cooking became stronger as we got closer to the house. A woman peered out of a door. "Come in, Fran," she said.

"Bill, your cousin Fran, and some of her friends are here," she yelled to someone inside. A voice from a distance called out, "Tell them to come on down." Fran led the way to the kitchen where Bill's wife was cooking. I could tell that everyone knew each other. Bill's wife talked to Al and the rest of the guys. Al said, "By the way, this is Charlie. He is in charge of the big cleanup for Standard Oil."

"Oh, he is? Pleased to meet you, Charlie, I'm Georgia. Come right in. You care for a cold one?" "Yes, thank you!" I said. "Coors is my favorite beer." Then Fran, who had sneaked away to talk to her cousin, came out of a room with Bill and said, "Come with me, Charlie. I want to introduce you to my cousin."

*"Man, what a house,"* I thought as Fran introduced us. All I initially said was, "I am glad to meet you, Bill. You have a warm house and it is beautiful."

I found out later that his parents gave the small estate to him as a wedding gift. Both Fran and Bill's parents were very well heeled; in other words, rich!

I reached into my pocket and handed Fran $300.

She said, "All right. Groovy. All this?"

I replied, "Why not? What time is it?"

Bill answered, "3:30."

"I don't have anything to do until 7:30."

Bill said, "We can sit by the pool and relax."

I thought, *"What a good way to slow down!"*

Everyone retired to the pool. We had a good evening just talking and eating great food; 7:30 came too soon. We made arrangements to meet there whenever I had a problem in the community. Also, I understood that this was where the cocaine bag was!

I knew I had the town sewn up. I also knew I had knocked Fran; she started acting as my secretary.

"Charlie, it is 7:30."

I said, "Let's get together later. I am staying at the Seadrift, rooms twenty-eight and twenty-nine. Call me around 11:00 tonight."

"Okay," everyone said goodbye as I made my way back to my car. I really felt good and I was a little high!

As I drove up Highway 101 past the little restaurant, a line was outside. All workers were furnished meals at our expense. As I pulled into a parking space, Chet and Stan ran out and asked, "Are you all right?"

I replied, "I can take care of Charlie."

Chet said, "Those kids frighten me."

I responded, "I love them. Now what's going on, Chet?"

"Where do you want me to start?"

"I don't know. Why don't we go down to this little café and have some coffee? We can start talking there.""Okay." At that point, Chet began to fill me in while we walked under the trees. "Let's pass by the beach," I suggested. As we did, I saw that Chet had nightlights set up. We were rolling and I mean rolling. "How many trucks do we have stockpiling?" I asked. "About seventy-five," Chet replied.

"Wow! What is my commission on each truck per hour?"

"About one-fifty."

"You mean a dollar and fifty cents for you and the same for me, Chet?" "Yes." Chet said, "The way I figure it, on all the equipment you and I make about three hundred and fifty per hour each, allowing for all the problems and expenses that come up unexpectedly. On the other side, every ten hours you and I each have a profit of $3500, plus we make money on other things, but all that is soft. My wife, Adell, and Claudia are setting up books as fast as they can. We hired seven new office people and two outside CPAs."

"Good. By the way, make my wife Personnel Director and pay her $500 per day. In return, she will sign my checks in case I am not around. As far as your daughters and wife are concerned, they are on my wife's staff. Pay them $750 a day because they are on-call twenty-four hours a day. Now, about the job: this is a Walker Trucking project. All bills and bank accounts should start to read that way. By the way, Chet, it is going to take all my energy to keep the lid on this town."

"Let me tell you, Charlie, at the meeting with Standard Oil this morning, the executives thought you were God. I must say, I never thought you had that much talent."

"Really, Chet, you sure have a way with words, no shit."

"Charlie, the moment you appeared, all those youngsters just seemed to melt at your feet, but that enabled us to do the cleanup."

I didn't respond to Chet's last remark, but I continued to mull over it as we walked toward the café. I was somewhat flattered by Chet's comments, but deep down I knew better than to trust the words of a man known for lying and empty words.

We entered the café. As I entered, it got quiet. I could see that everyone was looking at me; I could feel their eyes closely watching me. People started speaking to me and saying, "Hi, Charlie." As I looked around, I knew I was the only black person within twenty-five miles. However, it seemed like I was the only black person on earth. The situation gave me a strange, isolated feeling.

The restaurant owner soon emerged from behind the bar. "So you are Charlie! Goddamn. Why didn't anyone tell me?"

I interrupted, "Nobody told you." I laughed along with everyone in the place. We all knew what we really wanted to say.

Then he said, "Let me buy you a drink."

"Good," I said. "rum and Coke."

Chet and I stood at the bar. Five people offered us their table, but I refused. I knew everyone in there worked for me. My mind was running on fast-forward. At times, I would replay in my mind events that happened to me because of my color. I reflected on how unimportant it was at that moment. People respected someone who produced, regardless of skin color. I experienced a producer's thrill because I felt like a part of the people and the town.

Finally, we got a table. Chet ordered a steak for himself and I informed him that since I had eaten earlier, now I'd have coffee and perhaps a dessert. By that time, both of us had forgotten how we first met. Now we were working as one pair, not apart! After reflecting on our working relationship, I told Chet, "Look, I need to keep about $5,000 around and I want you to hire about fifteen people. They will work directly for me."

Chet said, "That makes good sense."

"I want to find out what we owe these people at this café and pay them. Also, rent five vans and put one at their disposal. Also, we must help them in any way we can, even if it means advancing them money. Don't dog them down with checks and don't ask them for anything. Only ask, 'How much money do you need?' They are honest people. Please don't let anyone handle this but you." Chet said, "Don't worry. I will handle it."

I continued, "Now, I need three rooms at the motel down the street. In fact, rent the whole motel as we have the Seadrift."

"Okay," he said. "We have a very important meeting tomorrow morning at 8:30 with every important person from Standard Oil." "All right. You and I are going on a tour in the chopper at 7:30

tomorrow morning so we will be ready for them. Have Chuck here at 7:00 tomorrow morning and you wake me up at 6:45. In the meantime, I am going on a little run. Give me a couple hundred dollars."

Chet said, "It just so happens that I am currently running on empty."

"Okay, never mind. I'll see you later."

# History 5

# "Tired"

I went straight to the bed, lay across it, and fell asleep; I did not realize how tired I was. I thought I had just lain across the bed, but when I got up to go to the toilet, it was 3:30 a.m.. I pulled off my clothes and went back to bed.

A loud knock on the door soon woke me from my light sleep a few hours later. I had been thinking something had to be done about the beach because it was not cleaning up as everyone thought it should. There was another loud knock at the door, which woke me to full awareness. As I touched the doorknob, a loud pop went off in my head.

I said aloud, "I know, I know, I know." I opened the door saying, "I know, I know." Stan Smith, the field supervisor for Standard Oil, was at the door.

I stood in front of him saying, "I figured it out." "Figured what out, Charlie?"

I said, "I figured out what everybody is doing wrong. I figured out how this job has to be done. Where is the chopper?"

"On the beach," Stan said.

"I need it right now."

"Hold it," Stan said.

"There are two men from the Labor Department here to see you."

I said, "Go tell them you just missed me and tell Chet to meet me at the helicopter." "But, Charlie…" Stan tried to say. I interrupted, "Fuck those guys. I have something to do that is much more important."

"But Charlie, you have to see these guys."

"Look Stan, just do what I ask you and tell them, whoever they are, I'll be back in a few minutes. Take them to breakfast. Get them drunk. Get them some girls. Do anything, but get Chet to the helicopter. Entertain those two assholes. I am going to do something that is going to make us lots of money."

"Okay, I'll take care of it."

He finally left. I got dressed and ran to the chopper, piloted by Chuck, the best pilot Standard Oil had. Chet was already sitting in the back seat. I just jumped in and said, "Take off quick."

Chet asked, "What the fuck is wrong?" I started laughing and said, "Nothing, Chet. How did everyone overlook this?" Chet impatiently asked, "What? What in the hell are you so excited about?"

"I am going to show Standard Oil a trick. Chuck, I am going to Chet's yard where we went the first day we met."

"Roger, Charlie."

We were on approach. As we passed over Candlestick Park, I saw what I was looking for: three paddle scrapers. "I am right, Chet. You see those paddle scrapers of yours?" As soon as I said it Chet started laughing and said, "You are right, Charlie, you are right." Chuck said, "Would someone let me in on the secret?" Chet said, "It's no secret. Charlie just thought of something no one else did."

"Look Chet, don't tell anyone. Put them on lowboys and get them up there as soon as possible. When do you think the first one will arrive?" "Well," Chet said, "It's 9:20 now. At 1:00 p.m. I will have it on the beach." "Good," I said. "I'll see you there." Chet climbed out. I said, "Take me back, Chuck."

As we were landing back at Stinson Beach, I could see an ocean of equipment.

I thought to myself, *"All these people are working for me. It is 10:50 a.m.. I wonder who these clowns from the Department of Labor are."* As soon as we touched ground, I ran to the office. When I opened the office door I saw two white men who looked like police officers, wearing wing tip shoes. I called them the shoes with a thousand eyes because of all the little holes in them.

As the door closed behind me, both of them stood up as if they were mad. They were. "Mr. Walker," one said as he was opening a little folder in his hands. "Yes, may I help you?"

The other snotty one said, "No, we are here to serve you notice, also Standard Oil, that no one, but no one, can work for free in the state of California unless they willingly volunteer to aid in natural disaster relief efforts. However, both of those ships belonged to Standard Oil, so Standard Oil, as a corporation, is solely responsible for dealing with this mess and must fully compensate all employees; businesses can't have volunteers! I want you to hear me and hear me clearly. Everyone, and I mean everyone, who is working or has worked, must be paid, volunteers or not."

At that point he served me a handful of papers. I did not notice that Shard and other Standard Oil and Industrial Railway employees were standing in the doorway as I was getting the Riot Act read to me. When they finished talking, the Labor Department men stormed out of the room. As soon as they turned their backs, I looked intently at the back of their heads, and shrugged my shoulders. I then called a meeting with everyone for 2:00 and gave instructions to all foremen, supervisors and office personnel to provide any records they had of people who had volunteered.

At that meeting, I found out that no one had kept records and we would just have to ask people if and when they started volunteering, relying solely upon their word. As I expected, nearly everyone in the town, far more than the couple of hundred volunteers we actually had, showed up and said they had volunteered since day one and demanded payment for their work. Standard Oil spent thousands of dollars paying people who claimed to be volunteers who in reality

55

just saw an easy opportunity to get some cash. Standard Oil got screwed over, but Tennat, the one who was everybody's boss had told me initially to spend money and that's just what I was doing.

After the Department of Labor representatives left and I scheduled a meeting in the afternoon, I realized that Chet was on his way with the paddle scrapers. I walked over to the ocean while I was waiting for Chet and the executives from Standard Oil to arrive. Oil was permeating everything. Chet and I really did not have a game plan; we were still getting organized.

As I looked to the right, I could not believe my eyes. I saw three helicopters rapidly approaching as if they were invaders from who-knows-where. Each chopper had a cable strung down holding three fifty-five gallon drums. I could not imagine what was in them, but it did not take long to find out.

As the result of someone in Standard Oil hitting the panic button and someone else saying that mineral oil could clean the crude oil off the wild life when mixed with butter, all day long the three choppers brought in mineral oil and six tractor-trailers forty feet long bringing in butter.

While I stood on the beach looking at the same mountain I drove down when I first entered the quaint little community three days before, a convoy of equipment arrived. The side of the trailers read, "FOREMOST." I thought, *"Huh, I ordered something from a dairy?"* I learned a few minutes later that Standard Oil had ordered it for me. That was part of the butter shipment. Now I had tons of hay to suck the butter up from the sand, enough mineral oil to work the world if it was constipated and butter from half the cows in Texas! As I entered the office, someone handed me a bill of lading for 144,000 pounds of butter and 47,500 gallons of mineral oil. I signed it like I knew what I was signing. I said to myself, *"This is the largest corporation in the world. How in the fuck did that happen?"*
"Charlie! Charlie! Charlie!" Shard called.

I was daydreaming and just thinking as I absentmindedly

replied, "Yes, Shard."

"Look Charlie, we need to talk."

"About what?"

"Well, everyone is working at first one thing and then another. What real progress are we making?"

"Well, you'll see as soon as Chet gets down that hill, if you look up there," I said.

He said, "Where?"

"Right there."

As I pointed up the mountainside, Shard inquired, "What the fuck is that?" I said, "The answer to the question you just asked."

"What question did I just ask?"

"Aren't you the same person who just asked, 'When are we going to start showing some progress?' Well, here comes progress." He scratched his head and asked, "What is that?" I said, "Let's just call it progress. By the way, when will the president of Standard Oil arrive?" "Oh, that's why I was calling you. He'll be here at 2:30 sharp." "Good," I said. "I will have a demonstration for him. He is going to think I am 'Super Nigga!'" Everyone in the office laughed. As I turned around, a young lady answered the phone. I asked, "What is your name?" "Mr. Walker," she replied, "I am June." "Well, June," I said, "You are my secretary from now on. Whom do you work for, first and foremost?" "You," she replied. I said, "Who hired you?" She said, "Mrs. Smith." I said, "Good." I knew if Adell, Chet's wife had hired her, she was sharp.

"Get your pad and pen and when this meeting starts, just follow me around as if you have been my secretary since Moby Dick was a sardine."

She laughed and jumped to her feet.

"However," I said, "whatever you do, don't talk or ask questions during this meeting." She looked mystified.

I said, "The reason is if you don't say anything, people won't know anything." She smiled and said, "Okay!" I looked over toward the parking lot. Chet and Willie, the operator, were unloading the paddle scrapers.

I felt very secure because I knew this was the trick. Willie backed the scraper onto the beach. Some of the employees in the nearby vicinity stopped to look at Willie and the paddle scraper. I knew that it must look strange on the beach with its large four wheels and big central compartment, jokingly referred to as its "belly." I put on my hard hat and ran over as Willie started in a forward motion. I waved him to a stop. I told him I wanted him to make a pass at the water's edge. It was just my luck that as Willie started to make his first pass, the result was beautiful. He made a path through the oil and left a clean strip of golden sand.

It was as if someone took a razor down the middle of a person's head and made a clean swipe. The contrast of the small strip of dazzling bright sand through the enormously thick mass of oil was a remarkable sight. When I looked up, two choppers were hovering above and I could see that one guy had a camera. They eased to a soft landing just ahead of me.

I immediately ran over to my operator and said, "Look Willie, go all the way up and turn around. Dump as you turn." While I was talking, I could see three men approaching from the corner of my eye. I backed away as Willie pulled off toward the water. As I turned around, the three men were already upon me. Even if I hadn't previously met Tennat, the space that the other executives gave him wouldn't have made it difficult to identify the president of Standard Oil. "Hi, Mr. Walker." "Hi, Mr. Big Boss."

He laughed while saying, "Now this is my kind of guy." I extended my hand and he did likewise; our hands clasped. I said to myself, *"Now I understand. This man has the coldest hands I have ever felt in my life."*

"Look, Charlie, all I have heard of you is good. Another thing, you are the only one I have seen since the accident that appears to be making progress. As far as I am concerned, I have seen enough. I just left San Francisco and they have been working a day longer than you and you are the only one removing oil. Congratulations. Do you need anything?" "Yes." "What is that?" he said. "Petty cash," I said.

Tennat said, "You can have anything you want. However, I will take care of that personally. I will see you later." He didn't say another word. He turned and walked, almost running, to the helicopter. Everyone in the office was looking at him as he lifted off. One helicopter was much larger than the other. However, he was piloting the smaller one. He swung around and waved. The larger helicopter lifted off and they both were gone. At that point, an inner voice brought to my attention that he didn't ask about anything or anyone. One of the employees that had been standing around and watching the entire scene walked up to me and asked, "How did that thing do that?"

I explained, "It's a paddle scraper. The paddle scrapes up the top two inches of dirt, in this case oil and sand. The oil only seeps a half-inch down into the sand, so the paddle scrapers gets all the oil. Then it scoops it into the belly where it is ground up. The ground oil and sand sits in the belly until the operator prepares to dump it somewhere. Simple huh?" He looked dumbfounded and said, "Sure." I laughed and turned toward the office. As I walked back to the office, Shard opened the door and asked, "Where is Mr. Tennat?" I casually replied, "Oh, he left." Obviously surprised, Shard said, "He left?" I kept walking. "Yes," I said. "By the way, find Chet, Stan and Dan. I want to meet with all of you."

Shard turned away to look for them. I went into my office and sat down. I thought, *"Man you are on a roll. Everything is a go."* The requested employees stepped in one after another. Chet spoke up right away and asked, "What's up?"

I burst into laughter while they stood looking in amazement. All of them, almost in harmony, asked, "What happened out there?"

I said, "Chester, I need you to call Bob Fontana, David

Denardi and O.C. Jones, or whoever you have to, but tomorrow I want at least nine more paddle scrapers and six two-and-a-half yard long, rubber-tired loaders. I want them at any cost. In other words, Chet, I know you are charging $40 an hour operating and maintenance plus six additional dollars for our commission, at a total cost of $46 per hour. I also know that is on the high side. However, that does not matter. I will pay up to $60 an hour. For my part, I want $50 an hour on everything. There are no exceptions."

Chet replied, "I will have everything here by 7:30 tomorrow morning. Is that all?" I laughed and said, "That's it." All of them laughed. Shard shook his head and said, "You really have juice, Charlie." I replied, "We are doing a good job. I would be nothing without Chet and the rest of you.

"Chet, I want to talk to you before I go run some errands. Never mind a talk, I want you to go up and down the coast in the helicopter, and tomorrow morning we are going to have an organizational meeting. I want you to set down at RCA Beach because we have to clean up the oil that is there."

Chet bewilderedly said, "I didn't know we were going to go that far up." "Oh, I meant to tell you about that last night." I observed a little resentment growing in mid-level and higher Standard Oil employees. They seemed bothered by taking orders from a black man, and I made it very clear that I was in charge, and that I gave orders to my employees; I didn't give them any slack. I was getting to a point where I had to let some of those white boys know this was about beach complexion, not skin complexion. I had started to feel eyes enviously watching me. As a black man in America, I quickly learned that eyes could deliver feelings that people would never dare to verbally express. At that precise moment, I abruptly said, "I am going to have a drink. I'll be at the place down the street."

I suddenly became upset with everybody. Thinking about my skin judgment and that kind of bullshit depressed me. I often wondered why I could get along with young whites, but with whites my age or older, I always had problems. *"Fuck this!"* I thought. *"Go have a drink and crank up."* Five minutes later I was in the bar and it was packed. As I looked around, I saw people pointing at me. I heard some of them say, "He is the big boss. He's in charge." Frank, the owner, saw me and said, "Thank you for the money, Charlie." I replied, "I know every meal you are serving is for us. There is a union rule: if men are kept twenty-four hours or work over twelve hours, you must feed them at the employer's expense. So, if you need money, transportation or helpers at our expense, just tell Chet Smith." "Yes, Charlie. I sure needed a boost in life. God has sent me what I prayed for." "I am glad your prayers were answered." "The Man upstairs took care of me pretty well," he said. "Would you care for a drink, Charlie?" "Why not?"

After a few drinks, I thought about many things, but mostly how much my life had changed in just a few short days. All of a sudden, Chet came in the door yelling, "Charlie!" "Yes?" "Your wife and children are here." "Good," I said. "Frank, guess what?" "What's that Charlie?" "God must be letting the other part of the world go unattended." "Why is that, Charlie?" "Well, I was just thinking about many things and God was listening." "He was? What did he do this time?" "Well, he sent my wife to take care of me." We both laughed aloud. "See you later, Frank."

I ran up the road until I could see Yolanda (Landi), my oldest daughter. *"Landi is sprouting up like a weed!"* I thought. The kids saw me and started running towards me. The best feeling I ever had was seeing my children run towards me full of love and admiration. I couldn't help but think, *"America, what a great place!"* All three of them: Landi, Pookie and Dee Dee were talking at the same time saying, "We saw you on television." "You did?" Dee Dee said, "You sure looked dirty, Charlie. You know what Ann said?"

"No, what did she say?" Dee Dee said, "She said, 'Look at Charlie. I'll bet he smells just like that oil,'" while she pinched her nose in imitation of her mother. Landi said, "She was right. You do smell like oil." Pookie said, "I don't care. Pick me up and let me ride on your back." Ann walked up and said, "Get off my husband." I put the kids down and hugged and kissed Ann. We walked to the parking lot and everyone just stood around looking at my children, wife and me. Ann asked, "Why are all these people staring at us?"

I said, "Never mind. Let's go up to my motel. By the way, did you bring me some clothes?" "Yes," she replied. "Oh, I also heard that you have been talking about me," I said with a mischievous smirk. "Your children talk too much," Ann replied. I replied saying, "I know."

Chuck walked up and I introduced him to my family. My children were very friendly and instantly took to Chuck. Chuck kneeled down and talked to them. After what seemed like a few seconds, the girls asked, "Charlie, can we go with Chuck? He is going to take us for a ride."

"Chuck," I said, "where is Chet?" "He just left with Shard. They took the other chopper and went to RCA." I said, "Good. I was supposed to go run some errands, but they can wait."

Chuck said, "Boss, why don't you visit with your wife and I will take care of the kids." I said, "Okay." Then playfully eyeing my girls suspiciously I said, "Look you guys, if you cause Chuck any problems, I'll get that ass when you get back."

"Okay, we'll be good," they said in unison. The girls ran to grab their jackets and some gum from Ann. While Chuck and I were alone, he asked, "If you don't mind me asking, why do your kids call you by your first name?"

I laughed and answered, "Because my name is Charlie and my wife's name is Ann. I don't think there's anything wrong with using 'mama' or 'papa,' but it only feels right when people call me Charlie."

He said, "Oh," as the girls ran back, grabbed his hands and led him away. I took Ann to the beach and showed her the progress

62

we were making. Willie was still operating the paddle scraper and cutting small strips through the blobs of oil. Ann was astonished to see the relatively tiny streaks of golden sand compared to the expansive mass I was still fighting.

We then walked back to my room and made love. We spent the rest of the afternoon just filling each other in on what was happening. Ann told me how her mother and the girls were doing; I gave her a detailed update on the job. We lounged around until about 7:30 that night when Ann asked, "Where are my children?"

As soon as the words left her mouth, we heard the pitter-patter of Chuck and the kids running down the catwalk. Ann and I got up. She went into the bathroom to get dressed. After putting on my pants, I opened the door. The girls ran in telling me about the helicopter ride. They went over Candlestick Park, saw our house and all the bridges: the San Francisco Bay Bridge, Golden Gate Bridge, San Mateo Bridge, San Rafael Bridge and the airport, after which Chuck landed and bought them hamburgers.

After I thanked Chuck and the girls settled down, Ann and I finally got fully dressed. Ann prepared to go home and we began to walk to the car, my girls following. Around 9:30 p.m., Ann called and said she had arrived safely. I turned over and went back to sleep. I woke up at 5 a.m., got dressed and called Chuck, Chet, Shard, Dan and Stan. I later called Chuck back and told him to get the other chopper because all of us were going for a little trip. My intuition told me that today was going to be a very exciting day. If not, I was going to create some excitement.

I went to the office and heard equipment working on the beach. Everyone promptly arrived in a "What's the problem?" mood wondering why they had been summoned. I told Chet, "Go to the beaches and get all the foremen and supervisors. I want to talk to everyone."

He left and returned with nine other men in less than ten minutes. Some I knew; others I had seen, but did not know by name.

63

I said, "Please be seated wherever you can find a seat. Some of you I don't know by name, so please excuse me. However, that is not too important. After this meeting, I will get acquainted with those of you whom I don't know.

"Now that the formalities are taken care of, good morning! Let me start off by saying I met with the president of Standard Oil yesterday. I am going to give you an overview of how he feels. He is happy with our progress. We must take care of the townspeople by being polite, exercising courtesy and driving slowly in town. If there are any complaints, I want them brought to either Chet's or my attention. I am going to set up a desk with someone to just take complaints.

"Look, I don't want to change anything. Chet is running the job outside and on the beach. I am in charge of planning our strategy and handling all business. However, I have been noticing a little bullshit. I would like you to tell anyone who doesn't like my tan that I said he or she does not have to work here.

"Now that that has been said, let's keep this job rolling! As of this minute, regardless of what each man in this room is making, he gets a five-dollar an hour raise. Starting tomorrow, we are going to have a helicopter crew. Stan Smith is going to be in charge of it. We are going to clean those ravines all along the coast by hand. Chuck is going to be the leader for the helicopters. Chet will set up all the crews. I like the progress with the paddle scrapers. We are moving. Chet, we are going to start to haul out tomorrow. I understand we have about thirty or forty trucks. I am going to need close to a hundred trucks."

Chet said, "What?"

I said, "Yes. Also, we are going to have three rubber-tire loaders working twenty-four hours a day. In ten days from now, I want to see a lot more progress. Standard Oil wants progress; the people in this town want progress and we are going to deliver. Thanks, men. Let's get back to work!"

As everyone filed out, I heard one guy say, "He is not a bad guy." However, one man hung back. I turned and said, "What is your name, and what can I do for you?"

"Joey Samson is my name," he said with a very heavy southern accent. "May I talk ta ya in private? "I said, "Sure." We stepped into a side office and I closed the door behind us. "By God, I jus' wanna say I neva liked you people, but I wuz wrong. Kin I shake ya hand?" I said, "Why, it would be a pleasure." As he turned to walk out of the office, he had tears in his eyes.

I asked myself, *"What did I do?"*

Chet walked up to me as Joey left.

"What was that all about?" Chet asked.

I replied, "Nothing.  He is a nice guy."

As I proceeded to walk past Chet, he looked confused!  I laughed as I looked over my shoulder. "Let's go to breakfast, Chet." Chet began to question me all over again. "Charlie, what did that asshole want?" I said, "You would not believe it if I told you." Chet said, "Try me."

"He said that he has never worked for better men than you and me, and he thinks the world of you."

Chet said, "What?"

I said, "Let's go eat."

We walked to the restaurant. As we walked in, Frank said, "Hi boys." We replied, "Breakfast, and we want you to fix it." Chet said while pointing at me, "He is the best in town.  Fix us your specialty." Frank said, "For you two, I'll do just that."

We sat and talked about the entire job.  I told him everything from soup to nuts.  He brought me up to date on our commissions. I told him we had petty cash and progress payments coming today.

"When the first progress payment comes, I want our commissions off the top.  After that, tell your wife to cut checks."

The food arrived hand delivered by Frank.  What a breakfast! "Frank, this is it!  Hot biscuits, preserves, eggs, steak, hash browns,

65

blueberry muffins, milk, coffee, brown gravy and a stick of butter. Thank you, Frank," I said. Boy, was it good!

That day, the fifth day, went smoothly. I stayed on the job and didn't encounter any problems. I also received money, paid bills and went to the bank. On the sixth day, the job continued to roll along without any kinks. I woke up on the seventh day unable to believe my luck. I swore that the past six days were a dream because things were going too well. I was making money so fast that it was unbelievable! I was getting over $5,000 an hour. Despite my slight apprehension, I had the feeling that the day was going to be amazing and it was! I could never have imagined how amazing it would eventually turn out. Since I had decided to use the paddle scrapers, the mixture of oil and sand was being hauled away at a rapid rate. As the owner of the job, I owned everything that I hauled and by then I had several hundred thousand yards of sand and oil. I had trailers parked on the outskirts of town full of the mixture and had to continually order more trailers to hold all the oil that was being hauled away.

Also, my experience in the trucking business turned out to be even more useful. After working with different contractors for a while, I randomly learned that asphalt was nothing more than sand and oil with a rubber base to make it harden. Surprisingly enough, beach sand was the best sand in the world to use when making concrete. So the oil that was a nuisance and an eyesore to everyone else was in reality thousands of gallons of liquid money - beautiful diamonds in the rough!

That day, a concrete factory owner contacted me about buying the sand and oil mixture. We reached an agreement and I sold it to him for a dollar a yard.

So on top of my commission, I was making money off the job that I was making money off - it was great! The job's progress was incredible and we were rolling twenty-four hours a day. Everything was smooth!

# History 6

# "Day Eight"

When I arrived on day eight, I noticed a large crowd forming on the beach. I immediately ran down and jumped through the crowd. Everyone stood around an injured person. "Stand back," I yelled. Chet was right behind me. I heard him say, "Stand back. We called the medics." I yelled, "How did this happen?"

It was a young white kid. He looked clean cut. His leg was twisted in such a manner that I knew it was broken. He was in pain; he was also sweating profusely. I took off my jacket and wrapped it around him. "Chet, go get me a blanket."

Everyone from the office was behind me. When I looked up, I saw a highway patrol officer running toward us. Someone threw me a blanket while the patrolman jumped down beside me. People were coming from everywhere. It seemed like the ambulance was never going to arrive. Each minute seemed like an hour. The ambulance finally arrived, actually two of them. Someone had said that more than one person had been run over. It wasn't long before the kid was in the ambulance and gone.

I found out a few minutes later that the operator went to take a leak and left the motor running. I made it back to the office. Chet was trying to tell me about the operator. I said, "I don't give a fuck, get him off the job." I did not know he was standing behind Chet.

The operator said, "Those fucking kids had no business climbing up on my equipment." I replied, "And you didn't have any business leaving the motor running. You are fired as of this minute. Pay him, Chet. There is no reason to discuss anything. He is old enough to know better. Fuck all the talk."

As I turned to walk away, three people said, "Telephone."

I picked up the receiver and said, "Yes?"

"This is Tennat."

"Yes, Mr. Tennat?"

"What happened, Walker?"

"One of our operators left the motor running on his road grader. A teenager got on it, and ran over another teenager. I will give you a full report this afternoon."

"Fine, Walker. Is everything under control?" "So far, so good. I have to go to see about the kid that got ran over. I will call you when I return." "Okay," he said. I turned, ran out to my car and drove off in a rush. I didn't exactly know where the emergency center was located. I saw a telephone booth. I thought, *"Good."* I stopped, jumped out and called the operator. When I told her what I wanted, instead of giving me the phone number, she connected me to the hospital.

"Emergency," someone said. After I told them who I was, he gave me directions. I drove straight there. I double-parked and ran into the Emergency Room. In that little town, no one had to tell me that I looked a little out of place. As I walked up to the counter, a white woman pretended to be busy and started to turn away from me. When I was busy, I didn't tolerate race madness, and this was one of those times. Before I thought about it, all the ghetto in me came out.

"Where are you going, bitch?" I immediately had everyone's attention. "Look," I said, "where is the youngster who was run over on Stinson Beach? I am the owner of the equipment." As I said that, a man walked in asking about the kid. He turned out to be the teenager's father. He was delighted that I came to see about his son. We introduced ourselves. I told him how to get in touch with me. I also told him that Standard Oil would take care of anything the kid needed. He said he was very impressed with the way I responded. At that moment, almost in unison, a hundred young people showed up outside the hospital. After I finished my conversation with the father, I walked out into the street and everyone wanted to know how the kid was doing.

I stopped, gave a full report and answered questions just as if I was at a press conference. I liked press conferences.

After I said, "I am not Standard Oil or any other big corporation. I am interested in what happens around me," the response was astonishing.

Everyone applauded. As I looked in the crowd, I saw Fran. I shouted out, "Hi Fran." She approached saying, "Hi Charlie," and kissing me on the cheek. I was flattered. I stopped at my car. As I did, Fran jumped in the other side. I drove off quickly. She started explaining how she and her friends stopped a lot of unnecessary bullshit. They always listened closely to what the townspeople said and were on the lookout for negative sentiments. They also emphasized Standard Oil's progress and made sure everyone focused on how well we were cleaning up and not that the entire mess was our fault. She also told me there was a party in Bolinas that night at a little club. I agreed to come. It was at that point that she kissed me in the mouth. I laughed and said, "We will finish that tonight."

She replied, "Promises, promises, promises," and reminded me that I stood her up. It was then I remembered our 11:00 date.

I laughed and said, "I thought you were going to call me. Well, forget that and come by the Seadrift Motel around 9. We can go get some blow, go to the club and have lots of fun."

I headed towards the office. When I arrived in the parking lot, everyone was in a state of confusion.

71

All at once, a hundred people asked me how the kid was doing. I responded, "Fine, just a broken leg. He will be all right."

While I updated the staff, Fran leaped out of the car; I didn't see her or which way she went. Our whole work force was moving with trucks rolling. I stopped in the office. Adell Smith had moved next door to me. I walked over and turned in all of my records. As I walked in the door, a quick scan of the room gave me a count of seven people. Each one had a handful of ledger cards. When I walked in Claudia said, "Hi Charlie."

So I asked her, "How many people are employed by us on this job?" She laughed and said, "The last time I counted, 233 operating engineers, truck drivers and skilled craftsmen, 800 beach cleaners, and 160 beach cleaner supervisors and growing."

"Okay, we are not hiring any more beach cleaners. In fact, in about fifteen days, we are going to start laying off all beach cleaners, but we will talk about that later. This job is rolling along and should be done in a few months. Is everything stabilizing?" Adell said, "Well, yes. We will get everything in order in a couple of days."

While I was speaking to Adell, I asked, "Where is your husband?" She replied, "Who knows?" I said, "Well, I would like for us to take care of that accident."

Adell said, "Claudia is taking care of that. She called our insurance company. The piece of equipment belongs to us."

"Fine," I said. "Well, I guess that's all. Thanks everybody!" I left and returned to my office. I called Standard Oil and spoke to Mr. Tennat. We were both happy with the results. I explained that our insurance was covering the accident, but Chet's insurance would ultimately pay our insurance.

He said, "No problem. Remember, Charlie, we are the largest corporation in the world. I want you to spend money."

I couldn't believe what I was hearing. I said to myself, *"This guy has power."* I was already spending close to $50,000 a day.

I finally said, "Yes sir." The conversation was over and we

both hung up. I sat in my office dumbfounded. I thought, *"God, when you decide to give a person some money, do you always handle it like this? If so, no wonder most well-off people go crazy."*

The phone rang again. I said, "Yes, this is Charlie." The voice on the other end said, "This is Tennat again." "Yes, Mr. Tennat?" "Listen Charlie, can I speak to you very frankly?" "Yes, what can I do for you?" "Those kids over there like you, I understand." "Yes, I think so," I replied.

"Well, I want you to do whatever you feel is best, but keep them under control at any cost. Do you think you can do that?"

"I am pretty sure I can," I replied.

"Fine," he said. "Do you have enough money?"

I hesitated and said, "Well..."

He interrupted, "I am sending you some money by Chuck."

I said, "That is fine. What will I call it?"

He said, "Call it peace money!"

I laughed and almost choked.

He then said, "Remember, you are one of us now. I expect you to act the part."

I replied, "We won't have any problems."

I could not believe my ears. While we were talking, I heard a chopper landing. I figured, well, I didn't know what to figure. I only knew that I was a long way from Mississippi, smiling. "Thank you, sir. Chuck has arrived."

"Listen Walker, before you hang up, it is up to you to take care of our family." I replied, "I know my job, Mr. Tennat." Before he hung up he said, "I like your style. Call me anytime, and remember, you are in charge." "Thank you." We both hung up.

I jumped out of my chair a little confused, but I was somewhat comforted because I knew I had enough money behind me to do anything I wanted. I also knew that Tennat's power was at least one step beyond the norm, even for the president of a multi-billion dollar company. This man had too much power or too much money, but what difference did it make?  This was how America was run. This man's power was awesome.

I often thought of my father, thinking, *"Oh, if he could see me now."* I was sure he would have said, "That's the baddest boy I have ever seen."

While I was standing outside and talking to Shard who happened to be waiting outside of my door, as if he were listening to my phone conversation, Chuck entered my office.

"Hi Charlie," he said.

I replied, "Hi Chuck."

He handed me a large manila envelope.

I said, "Thank you very much."

Chuck said, "I have to go pick up those men in the ravines."

I thought, *"Men?  You mean tar babies.  Those boys go in pale and rosy and come out black as tar from head to toe."*

Everyone had a lot of respect for the difficult, tiring and dirty job the ravine workers performed.

I looked across the room and the clock said 4:36 p.m.  *"My, this day is shot,"* I thought.

Shard said, "Excuse me.  I need to have a talk with you Charlie." I said, "Chuck, go pick up your people and thank you for the package.

"Look Shard, I am going to be busy.  Can't you discuss whatever with Chet?"

"Well, I guess so," he said, obviously more than a little frustrated that his big concern wasn't important to me. I stepped back into my office and locked the door behind me.  I just knew this was cash.  Just call it peace money!  As I opened the envelope, I assumed that it contained maybe two or three thousand dollars.  I opened it and poured the contents on the desk.

*"Money, goddamn what the fuck is this?"* I wondered. I stacked the money, all hundred-dollar bills bank tied, into five neat little stacks. I couldn't believe my eyes.  I counted it as fast as I could

without taking it out of the wrappers. A fast count estimated the amount at $25,000.

*"Slow up,"* I said. *"This is just money to spend for no reason. Whom am I supposed to give it to and why? What for? Is this some kind of trap, but a trap for what? Well, I am in for all this shit."* I thought, *"Well, I am going to spend a lot of money on public relations. I am going to tell Chet almost all the facts. I am going to tell him that Tennat gave me twelve grand for public relations. I'll start another bank account and label it 'expense account.' If the subject ever comes up again, I will be able to explain, or even return any part of the other thirteen thousand."*

I said to myself, *"That bastard will have to get up much earlier just to trick me with some petty bullshit."*

I discussed it with Chet and told him about what had taken place with Tennat. He became suspicious too. However, he thought Tennat had only given me twelve grand.

I thought if it should ever come up again, since I didn't have to sign for it, I would just say, "That's all I received."

If necessary, I would cast suspicion on Chuck.

Chet said, "I think we should keep close tabs on this, so despite whatever he should say later, we will have an accurate record."

"Good," I replied. "Here, you take care of it. Remember yourself for all the expense money you have given me, like the day you gave me that money out of your wallet."

"Fine," Chet said.

"Also, give me $2,500 for expenses. I will give you a receipt now. I am going to some club in Bolinas tonight to play big spender to all the hippies. We don't want to have a problem with the townspeople after that accident today."

"Fine," Chet said. "That's your job, Charlie, and I must say you are good at it."

"Thank you, Chet, you are good at what you do also."

75

Chet counted out twenty-five one hundred dollar bills. I acted as if it was nothing, folded the money and crammed it in my front right pocket.

Chet said, "By the way Charlie, did you notice?" "Notice what?" "I had some of my compeers who were just standing around the beach wash your car."

I casually said, "Thanks," and without another word walked out of the office. I got in my car prepared to drive to San Francisco. However, I happened to glance at Chet before I drove off. He had a disappointed and somewhat angry expression on his face. I knew he didn't like me blowing off his favor.

I thought, *"Oh well; business is business,"* and drove away. As I passed the most beautiful scenery in the world, all I could think about was that my wife and children could have anything they wanted. I didn't care what it cost. I had never seen so many hundred-dollar bills in my life and they were all mine to use as I pleased. What a sensation; a high unlike any I ever felt before. I could pay off every bill we owed. I could let Ann buy something for herself and pay cash. I could take my children out on a shopping spree. I liked to buy gifts for children. I truly enjoyed seeing little children happy because they had an innocent, happy smile that genuinely said, "Thank you."

As I pulled up to the Golden Gate Bridge toll plaza, I handed the toll collector a $5 bill and said, "Buy yourself a drink when you get off today."

He looked at me, smiled and said, "Hey, you are my kind of guy." It seemed as though I had been only driving for about five minutes when I pulled up in front of my house on Goettingen Street. I was running on autopilot; I drove home without even realizing it!

As I walked in, I shouted, "Ann, Ann." She ran from the rear of the house yelling, "What's wrong? What's wrong?" I fell down in a chair and said, "You don't want to believe this, or you won't believe it." She replied, "Oh, I already don't believe you. Now show me what I won't believe."

I poured all the money on the coffee table. There was so much of it that some fell on the floor. Her eyes grew wide while she said, "You are right. Whatever you tell me I won't believe it, and I don't want to go to jail. About this money, I don't care how much it is, my children mean more to me."

"Well," I said, "May I explain?" Meanwhile, Ann called Rudy, her mother. Rudy lived just a few blocks away. She arrived a few minutes later. Ann and I were in the living room. When Rudy rang the doorbell, Ann ran over and opened the door. Rudy saw the money as soon as she closed the door behind her.

"My God, son," she said. "Who died and left us all this?" We all laughed. I said, "Rudy, would you sit down?" By this time, all the children were sitting around waiting to hear the money story. I never excluded my children when I talked about business, but one thing I insisted on was that they didn't open their mouths. At no time could they talk when business was being discussed.

"Let me tell all of you the straight-up on this." I told them what Tennat, Chuck and I had done. I told them the complete story and even shared my suspicions. I also told them what I did with Chet and the money I gave him. The moment I finished, Yolanda, my oldest daughter, said, "Excuse me, Charlie, may I say something please?" I reluctantly said, "Yes." "All of us know you would not get us in trouble. Now, can we spend some of it?" Everybody laughed.

Ann said, "How do you know? You are so much like Charlie; I wish you were born a boy. By the way, shut up. You are getting too grown up."

I could not say anything to Ann or Yolanda because of a rule. If Ann or I corrected a child, the other couldn't comment regardless of whether the other was right or wrong.


I told Ann I had to go back to Stinson Beach and that she should pay off our second mortgage even if she had to pay a penalty for paying it off early. I told her to save some money and get the kids and her mother whatever they wanted. I picked up eighteen one hundred dollar bills and said, "Duty calls."

# History 7

# "Fran glad to see me"

I left and drove back up to Stinson Beach. As I was pulling up, I looked at my clock and realized that it was 8:45 p.m..

"Wow," I said as I almost ran over Fran in the parking lot. She ran over, opened the door, jumped in the car and said, "Am I glad to see you."

As I looked around, I could see the job was in full force. Chet waved as he and five operators headed toward the beach. Equipment was everywhere.

Fran said, "We have been waiting for you."

I replied, "Good. I am ready Fran."

"Are you going to get some 'you know what?'"

"Are we talking about blow?" I said.

"Right on baby. How much?"

"Let's get an ounce," I said.

"What?" she asked. "Are you going to party all night?"

"You bet we are," I said. "I want the best he's got. What's it going for?" "$1,450," she said.

She jumped out and went over to the car she was sitting in before I arrived. I saw her cousin smiling. He got out and he and Fran got in my car.

"Let's go up to my house," he said.

We drove up to his house. It was a clear night and the weather was warm. It overlooked the ocean. My equipment was working with lights flickering and jumping and equipment cutting different paths through the oil. Every piece seemed to play its own melody and all of them came together in beautiful harmony.

Fran's cousin was a very smooth guy who never seemed to get excited. He didn't seem the least disturbed to sell coke; that was probably because it was the coolest recreational drug around at the time. I stuck my hand in my pocket and pulled the hundred dollar bills out. He set his triple beam scale and weighed twenty-eight grams, equal to one ounce. I gave him the money. Fran said, "Let's make up some gram packages."

I explained that I would like to give a gram to about seven or eight people who had been helping me. Fran understood. We put up the grams and left for the club. When we arrived, I found out that all the youngsters, including the one with the broken leg, were anticipating my arrival.

The club was packed and a small band was playing. That was the first time I met Buddy Miles. I didn't feel so bad; at least I wasn't the only brother around. In an arrangement such as that, no one looked at me because of my color.

Fran was all over the place. She was very well liked and well known. The staff set up a table for me with about eight or nine chairs.

Everybody came by and said, "Hello Charlie." I gave Fran a small package of coke. She was having a ball turning on all her friends. I gave the bartender a hundred-dollar bill and said, "Let me know when it runs out."

The club only sold beer and wine. I told him to put a pitcher of beer on every table and give everyone in the house a glass of beer. We were having a ball when two of Fran's girlfriends arrived, one black and the other white. They came over and sat down with us. Fran took them to the ladies room and gave them a hit of blow.

When they came back, their coats were removed. They had the prettiest bodies I had ever seen. I thought, *"Shit! These are the finest bitches in the world. If both of them fell dead right now, I would be willing to cook and eat them all by myself. I have seen some pretty women before, but they take the burnt cookies."*

The black chick was black, very black. The palms of her hands were blue. To add insult to injury, her name was "Black," and that's how she was introduced to me.

"Charlie," Fran said, "this is Black and Mae." I looked up and said, "I was going to call you Black. I wouldn't have cared what you said your name was." All of us laughed.

Black said, "I like him. This is the one you say is in charge of San Francisco?" Fran said, "Yes."

Fran had given me a promotion from a small to huge businessman. I didn't correct her.

Mae said, "I hear you have your helicopters and when you want to go someplace you go get your pilot and off you go. Is that true?" Everyone got quiet and looked at me. I said, "Well, somewhat." I loved every minute of it.

Mae said, "Fran, are all of you going over to my house after we leave here?" Fran said, "Yes."

Black asked, "Is Charlie going?"

Mae said, "Ask him."

I said, "Well, maybe I better not."

Mae said, "We won't bite."

I said, "I like biters."

We laughed.

Black said, "Well, are you going?"

I said, "Okay. Who will be there?"

Fran said, "Just the four of us."

I said, "Now, I like that." I knew that Fran told Mae and Black about the ounce of blow. I also knew that I was in for an evening that would be second to none. All of us snorted coke at the club. I gave Black and Mae a gram for their personal use. By the time we were ready to go, we had given away ten grams. I must have given everyone in the club a one-on-one because everyone was high.

Leaving, we went up to Mae's apartment, at least that's what I thought when she said, "This is my house and my parents gave it to me because I am a bad girl!"

I said, "I just love bad girls, and I am a bad boy. We make a good team."

Fran said, "I am the baddest of everyone here because I feel so hot." We parked and went in.

*"What a nice place,"* I thought. A long dish with straws was on the coffee table. I put seven grams of coke on the dish and had a hit. When I looked up, everyone was wearing an open-front negligee. I could not believe my eyes, but I still remained very cool. The three girls sat around me as if I was their man. I acted nonchalant as if I didn't see their nude bodies. All three were too beautiful.

Fran was more beautiful than I previously thought. They began to dance around me and kiss each other and me. I liked everything. However, I had mixed emotions when they started kissing each other. Fran said, "Let's all get comfortable and kick back." I thought, *"This Fran is a real bitch. She's giving me orders now. I am the man. I call the shots."* Then I said to myself, *"You are just high."*

When I looked up, Black and Fran were playing with each other on a small mattress they had just put on the floor. Fran put coke all over Black's black body.

Fran kissed her all over and Black moaned while saying, "Oh, ouch. Lick all of me baby." Then Mae said to Black, "We are going to do you all over." Black was really kicking up a fuss. Mae masturbated while sitting beside me with her eyes closed. She was breathing hard and sounded as if she was going to gag. She stuck her finger in the coke and then stuck the finger up in her as far as she could. She moaned and groaned. Black laughed while Fran licked her clit. Mae was in a frenzy masturbating. She was kicking like a chicken with its head cut off. Black and Fran were doing the sixty-nine. I was not sure I wanted to join in, but I saw some enjoyment in watching them. It went on and on.

Finally I said, "I got something to do."

Fran said, "Don't go. Let's all have some fun."

"Is there any more blow?" Black asked.

I put five grams on the plate again.

Black said, "You are so cool. Don't you like us?"

I said, "I love you, all three of you, but we all express ourselves in different ways."

Black said, "Right on!"

I wanted to go to bed with Black, but I thought Fran might get mad and Fran was the key to peace on the job. Besides, I saw Fran lick Black. I knew in those types of relationships it was okay to fool around on occasion, but one of the women always got mad. Fran would be most likely to get pissed off and I didn't need any problems. I made up in my mind to leave and to catch them one at a time and take them off. However, it never happened.

Before I left, I joked around with them and made sure that we were still friends. I also gave them the rest of the coke I had. I sure wanted to get it on with Black, but I felt Fran and Mae liked her too much. I found out that she was living there with Mae. I also found out a day later that Mae didn't like Fran making love to her woman. Fran told me how much she enjoyed having oral sex with Black and how she wished she could have eaten the black off her. I laughed and said, "Just think, if you were still trying to eat all that black off her, you would be there when the Titanic docked in New York Harbor."

On the ninth day, I signed some checks and work orders. I also answered the phone and thought about the previous night. I was trying to figure out why I didn't touch either of those bitches, as fine as they were.

That day I must have talked to everyone in the world; people called me from everywhere. That was also the day we found out that the air conditioners had gone out in the trailers containing butter parked a half-mile down the road. Under the warm sun, the butter quickly melted and began to ooze out of the trailers, down the tires and onto the road. The butter almost instantly began to smell and the wind gradually carried the stench to the office. Executives frantically ran around trying to locate the owners of the vehicles while also creating a cleanup crew. By noon, half the town had come to the office to complain of the smell.

We hurriedly worked to remedy the problem because no one wanted two major cleanup efforts going on at the same time. I suggested cleaning out the trailers with large drums similar to how workers cleaned out the ravines. Everyone approved and the butter was completely cleaned up that day. I worked until 11 p.m., left, went to my room and fell asleep.

The manager of the motel woke me up at 9:30 the following morning to ask me for $500. I got up, went down the hall and walked right into Chet Smith. I told him what I needed. He stuck his hand in his pocket and handed everything to me. As he was handing me the money, the manager walked up and I gave her $500. I went back to bed and dozed off. I was awakened by the telephone ringing several times. At 5:45 p.m., I heard someone running down the catwalk and then a loud knock at my door.

"It's Chet."

"Yes, Chet?" I answered.

As I opened the door, Chet said, "Every big wheel in the world is here. They are going to spend the night because they are going to have a press conference tomorrow morning."

I asked Chet if Tennat was with them.

"Yes," he replied.

"Let me get dressed and I will be right down."

Chet left. I took a shower, got dressed and walked down to the office. I could see we had a full staff working and the beach was lit up. As I stepped through the door, Claudia looked up and said, "Hi Charlie." I asked, "Where is everybody?"

Claudia said, "We are all here. My father, Mr. Tennat and some more men took the helicopter and said they were going to look at the beaches all the way to Half Moon Bay."

I remained in the office for two or three hours and then went down to the restaurant to eat and have a few drinks. It was around 11:00. The restaurant was about to close down to sandwiches and bar drinks only. As I was getting ready to leave, Chet and Shard entered.

Chet said, "Just the man we were looking for. Come over here and let me speak to you." Chet and I stepped away from Shard as Chet whispered, "I couldn't believe my ears, but it was old hat. All the big wheels were up here and they wanted to have some fun tonight; but they didn't want the nigger around." Chet didn't quite say it like that, but that was the point.

Chet said, "That's how people are. I used to be like that until I met you." "Let's get one thing straight, Chet. Believe me, I know those high level, almost rich bastards. I know what they like and I know what they do. So, what do they want?" Chet said, "Some girls." "Girls I don't have. I know people, but how shall it be paid for?" "I will ask them."

"That's alright. We can take it out of the public relations money. By the way, how many are there?"

"Six," Chet said.

"Well, I will line things up," I affirmed. I had mixed feelings about my participation, but I didn't want to cut off my money line. Just as I thought that, Fran walked through the door. She jumped around as high as she could be.

Fran said, "Hi baby. How are you? Or shall I say, 'How are you, Mr. Walker?'" "Fine, Fran," I said. "Look Fran, I want to talk to you. Let's step outside." We did and I saw Black and Mae were sitting in the car along with Fran's cousin. I pulled Fran to the back of the car and explained what I needed. She said, "Fuck them. We don't do that. We came to get you. We are going to hang out. Tell them to find their own women." I explained to her that I had agreed to help. She said, "My cousin can handle it." I said, "Why don't you talk to him for me?" She called him out of the car and told him. He smiled and said, "That's nothing. You could have told me, Charlie. Let me go use the phone."

In the meantime, Shard walked back up to the motel. Fran's cousin used the phone. As he walked back from the phone, he asked how many girls we wanted. Then he went back to the phone. He only said a couple of words and hung up.

When he returned, he said, "I have got to go pick up two of them." That's when I said, "Look, I have to run and pick up some money." I walked over to the phone and called Ann.

"Bring me $1,500. I have an emergency," I said.

I wasn't concerned about Ann getting mad because we already had an arrangement that I set up when I first started the job. She knew that she would only see me rarely while I was working. We also talked about the money I was going to make and I promised her I would not let the money change us; we knew that money wasn't everything. Additionally, Ann knew that when I was with her, I was with her one hundred percent. She and any other woman knew not to be concerned with what I did or with whom when I wasn't with them; it wasn't their business. Regardless, Ann knew that she and the girls were my priority, so she knew not to let all this other bullshit bother her.

I told her to drive across the Golden Gate Bridge and meet me at the Golden Gate Motel just outside of Sausalito. I took Fran, Black and Mae with me so that Fran's cousin could pick up the ladies of the evening. I told him to coordinate his action with Chet. I also told him that I would give him a hundred dollars for helping me. I met Ann at the spot. However, I dropped Fran, Black and Mae off about a mile behind me. I knew I could explain those women to Ann, but I wasn't going to try. Despite our arrangement, I knew how to avoid situations that could give rise to problems later on. Fortunately, everything went off like clockwork. When I arrived back at Stinson Beach, Fran's cousin had a carload of fine ladies. They looked like college girls. I was elated at how he performed. I thought to myself, "I ought to buy some of that," but business was business.

I got a price for everything.

Fran's cousin said, "The girls want a hundred dollars apiece." I asked, "What am I buying?" He said, "Whatever the guys want or want to do." I gave him $700 and told him he could get us a half-ounce of cocaine.

I added, "Also, tell those ladies of the evening that if they want some coke, I will furnish some."

After I said that, all of the girls said, "I like this job; it's first class."

One of the ladies said, "I like him. What is your name?" Fran said, "Never mind that, just do what you are hired to do."

I pulled Fran's cousin to the side and told him, "I really don't know why, but I played a wild card. I want you to check with the ladies or have them check and see if any of the executives use cocaine."

He said, "That's a good idea."

It turned out that all of the executives, including the president, messed around with coke. However, Chet didn't mess around. I knew that and made it clear to Fran's cousin that no matter what happened, he absolutely could not let Chet know about the drugs.

After I bought some coke for Fran and that bunch, I felt a little uneasy. My intuition told me that whatever happened that night would somehow be significant. I pushed those thoughts out of my mind and drove to my house in San Francisco and spent the night with my family.

# History 8

# "Day Eleven"

I returned to Stinson Beach around 7:30 a.m. on the eleventh day. I had never seen most of the people there; only Tennat had met me. This day had some real revelations. The first thing that went wrong was the motel owner had again loaned Dan Wakeman money the previous night. This time it was $750. As I got out of my car, she shouted, "Mr. Walker, I would like to talk to you."

I walked up to her office and she talked me up one side and down the other about some misunderstanding between one of my men and a woman and the loan to Dan. At that point I did not know if Chet had gone home after he had paid the girls, or anything else. No one knew about the public relations money except for the pilot, Tennat, Chet and myself. I also found out later that the $750 was for more drugs the previous night when all the executives and ladies of the evening had an orgy that turned into total madness. Additionally, I found out that one of the big wigs left the orgy and checked into the motel in Bolinas.

Some time had passed since I started the job; it was in the fast lane now. We were cleaning the beach on a twenty-four hour basis with equipment and trucks everywhere. It was nerve-racking to keep anything that involved a lot of people in high gear, but somehow we managed. Chet was a professional who knew the trade.

89

Dan Wakeman rushed up to me after I got away from the innkeeper and said, "Charlie, I have got to get you to sign some blank truck tags to cover the money I borrowed."

I said, "Why?"

He asked, "Do you know about last night?"

I already knew that when someone asked a question like, "Do you know what happened?" to reply, "Well part of it," because the person talking would usually say, "Well, this is what really went on," and then proceed to tell me the entire story. Dan did just that.

He told me about all the bullshit from the prior night. I said, "We will call pussy, 'trucks hauling dirt.'" Dan fell out laughing. As far as I was concerned at that moment, I didn't really care about what had happened. I didn't want to rock the boat because I was going to (and eventually did) get a progress payment for $350,000 that afternoon.

We continued to talk about the previous night when Dan abruptly stopped talking. His facial expression became grave as he seemed to remember something unpleasant.

After an extended pause, he said, "We were up in the room talking and Tennat said something really horrible, but everyone laughed for an hour, even the whores."

I sarcastically said, "Tennat said something inappropriate? No!" Dan said, "I think you should really know, but if I tell you, you might get mad."

"Mad? How could I get mad?"

Dan didn't respond to me, but just eyed me while apparently trying to figure out whether he should tell me. By that time, Dan had spent so much time building my suspense that I became impatient. I said, "Okay, you can tell me already."

He said, "Let's walk outside or go grab a bite to eat and on the way I will tell you all about it." I agreed and we left, walking in the direction of the restaurant.

It was a clear morning and the air was refreshing. A few

90

moments later, Dan said, "I really hope you don't find it too offensive."

My impatience was now bordering on anger because I never liked to be toyed with, which is what I felt like Dan was doing.

I irritably said, "Dan, if you don't tell me now, I will definitely be upset."

He shrugged his shoulders and said, "Okay." Dan removed a handkerchief from his rear pocket to wipe his brow as he had begun to sweat during the brisk walk.

He said, "They were all naked when I arrived at the motel. Well, all except for Tennat, he still had on his shorts. The reason I was called was because they wanted some money. Tennat called me and I told him that money was no problem. I borrowed the money from the landlady."

I asked, "Well, what was so wrong with that?"

"Well, I arrived at the door with the money. Tennat told me to come in and I did."

I said, "Well?"

Dan continued, "I had no idea what he was leading up to. I was inside and one executive was licking one of those broads all over. They were having a hell of a time. I felt so out of place."

I replied, "Why didn't you say, 'Just a moment,' and remove your clothes also?"

"I wouldn't think of doing that shit."

I asked, "What else?"

"Well, after I was inside, Tennat pranced around and said, 'Dan, maybe you can help us.'"

"Gladly."

"Well," he said, "can you tell us how a nigger got in charge of all of us?"

"Then everyone in the room looked up and in unison said, 'I didn't do it!'"

"I felt so stupid, Charlie. I didn't know what they wanted to hear. Then all of them started laughing again. I started to leave and that's when Tennat said, 'Mr. Wakeman?'"

"Yes," I said.

"Don't you like our company?"

"I told him, 'Yes, but I have to go to the office in about an hour. As you know we are terribly busy.'"

Dan continued, "That's when Tennat told me that if I still wanted my job as a force account contractor, it would be to my advantage to find out how we can make it appear to the press that one of us got everything under control. I asked, like a dummy, 'Who is us?' That's when it got out of control. He fell right out of his tree.

"Tennat said, 'Listen to me very carefully, Mr. Wakeman. Before you leave, this is what I want. This asshole Charlie,' he was all up in my face by then. He said, 'I want you to have a talk with Walker. Tell him we will do whatever he wants, but we want him to rescind his position.' I asked him if he wanted me to offer you money. He said he would get together with me after this press conference."

Dan continued, "As I stepped back, he slammed the door. What really pissed me off was that I could hear them laughing after the door slammed. I didn't know what to think. I didn't know how you were going to act or react. What I still can't figure out is, what difference does it make? I don't understand. I am white, but I don't feel that way, and why is there such a difference in the way people feel depending on skin color? How can a man in such a high and respectable position be like that? I really am truly disgusted. We have been authorized to pay you one progress payment. Oh, that's one thing I did not tell you. He said he was sure you would understand."

"Well, well, well, Dan, there's one thing all blacks should keep in mind. White men as a whole look at us as some type of obedient servant and most of them are brainwashed that way."

Dan said, "Charlie, why would you say that? I find that hard to believe."

"Well Dan, I understand why white people look at us the way they do."

"Charlie, would you explain that to me?"

"Yes, Dan. We have been subject to our women being raped, and victims of our language being prohibited to be spoken, and brainwashed with foreign religious practices. In short, I can sum all of it up with this example: Most Jews will not embrace Germans. But most black Americans will embrace any white man, because of lack of knowledge. Well Dan, I know what goes on on these shores of America, I know when I'm up to bat, and I know when to lay the bat down. I don't come cheap, but I'll be his nigga in the woodpile. I don't want to hear about it after this. Just go to the meeting and tell him what I said. Then he can get on with it now that the line is defined."

Dan left and I walked onto the beach. As I looked at all the equipment rolling - a helicopter hovering overhead, a barge out in the ocean, trucks, loaders, light fixtures, generators to power the lights at night and a fuel truck refueling all the equipment on the beach - I thought to myself, *"It's unreal, but it's real, and I'm going to do what I gotta do."* As I contemplated the entire situation, I mused, *"I have done my job well. If this is what I am dealing with, I guess I'll have to change my approach to dealing with Standard Oil."* I left the beach and walked up to the office.

When I arrived, reporters were milling around everywhere. A wide row of trees separated the highway from the beach. After leaving the beach, walking through the trees and stepping into the light, the contrast between the sunlight and shade of the trees was so strong that it was like stepping from darkness into daylight. I observed Dan standing in the doorway of the office. When he saw me, he walked quickly down the short steps and started toward me.

We met and Dan said, "I don't believe this, but I will tell you anyway. I don't want you to say anything, Charlie. Just listen. Tennat wants you to let one of the white supervisors take credit for putting this job together, taking care of all the public relations and calming down the hippies. In other words, you are not to have had anything to do with this in so far as anyone knows except in-house. Oh, he also said that if you do this you could keep the twenty-five grand."

"Hold it Dan," I said. "Let me explain how I hear this shit. Okay Dan, you tell this motherfucka I want to maintain my status as the job owner. I want him to pay me $200 a day for every day I am going to be involved with this job, past and present. I will get all my commissions on all equipment. Also, I want a progress payment every week. I want the money today and one other thing, Dan."

"What's that Charlie?"

"How would you like to be a nigga today?"

Dan replied, "Not just any nigger! I wouldn't mind being yours on any day!"

"Well Dan," I said, "I can't make up my mind. I had a problem being black last week because I was broke. Today I am having a problem because I am black. You know Dan, for the first time I really understand why it is - and will be - more difficult for my people to understand the business mentality. It's not solely personal or business; the two are very closely related. Unless you grow up in that atmosphere, it is almost impossible to adjust to it. One minute, you are a part of the family. The next minute, they can't stand the sight of you. All businessmen can inherently sense when you are in a position of weakness, so if they wake up one day and decide they want some ass, if you are near and weak or vulnerable, you are it. I think that is what most blacks don't understand, but so much for that, Dan. Go do it. I will enjoy getting this shit over with this asshole."

Dan returned in a few minutes. "He approved everything you asked for." As Dan and I stood there talking, I said, "Let's go back inside and sit down."

We walked back inside the restaurant. Dan pulled out a long white envelope from his inside pocket.

"Charlie," Dan said, "I don't believe this. This is hard-core racism. What difference does it make who is in charge?"

"It doesn't. I don't care one way or another, but Chet is mixed up in this shit."

Dan said, "I could tell you some things I didn't think much of the other day."

"I don't care. I picked up $350,000 from your office; that's why I had them make it out to me. If they play shit with me, I won't give them a dime of it."

"Charlie, just let me say these guys play for keeps."

"Good," I said. "So do I. If I just think one of those punks is frowning at me, my foot will be so far up his ass that when he dies, they'll have to bury me with him. Now, how much money did you bring me?"

"Charlie, you are getting sick with your craving for money."

"Well Dan, I think that's how it is done. In order to make money, one must develop a sick craving for it. It's not personal; it's just money."

I opened the envelope and looked at an Industrial Railway check made out to me for $23,000. I couldn't believe my eyes. Also, the public relations money and all the commissions from the equipment were mine.

I took the money home and told Ann to keep it. As I walked out, all my children ran out of the garage and really got next to me.

Dee Dee said, "Charlie, I bet you are going to go make some more money."

I smiled and said, "You know I got to pay the bills."

Landi asked, "What bills?"

Ann said, "We don't have no bills."

Pookie interjected, "Don't go make money. I got $3. I'll give them to you. Just stay home and play with us."

"Let's do it another day. I have to go."

I got in the car and drove off. The children had gotten next

95

to me. I asked myself, *"Is it worth it?"*

A voice in the back of my mind shouted, *"Yes!"*

I drove over to Chet's yard. The day was clear and pleasant with a gentle breeze circulating throughout the city. I opened the door to a barrage of "Hello Charlie."

I replied, "Hi everybody! Is Chet here?"

"No, he is on his way," someone replied.

I walked over to the radio and pressed on the short wave.

"Base to S-1."

"S-1. Is that you Charlie?"

"Yes, Chet," I answered.

"Meet me at the Bayside."

"Okay." I replied. "Base clear."

I said, "Well, I'll see you people later," walked out, got in my car and drove to the Bayside. As I was pulling in, Chet was getting out of his station wagon. I parked and got out.

"What's happening, Chet?"

"I am glad we got together before tomorrow morning. Let me tell you, you cut yourself a good deal."

We walked into the café, another one of those small businessmen stops where everybody knew everybody. San Francisco was not too large if you were a busybody like me.

"Hi Chet. Hi Charles," various people said.

We smiled and spoke. In the industry, word spread fast when one was making it happen for himself and others.

Chet and I found a booth in the back and sat. Both of us were tired. We ordered cocktails and just sat back. When the drinks arrived, we began to talk about how much money was owed to me, how much was owed to him and how he needed a hundred thousand dollars. I told him I would give him a hundred grand tomorrow. He smiled and started to open up. Chet went on to tell me how we were together, how he was keeping the job going for me and that he couldn't understand the bullshit Standard Oil was pulling.

I sat just looking at him and the way he stumbled while he was talking to me. I didn't know everything that Standard Oil was up to, but I knew that Chet was somehow involved. Chet was trying to instigate part, if not all of my conflict with Standard Oil for his own selfish motives. I sat there for two-and-a-half hours listening and trying to read into all the bullshit that he was handing me. I understood one thing above all: if he were not in it, why was he explaining? Only fools explain; businessmen say, "I won."

I heard him saying that he was taking the job from me. I also heard that I couldn't beat Standard Oil like he could. All he wanted me to do was stand aside and I would get paid. He and I were really reaching an understanding. In essence he said, "I am going to fuck you, but I am going to let you make money while I am doing it." I also expressed my understanding of our agreement, not directly, but I said enough so that Chet knew that we both knew what was happening.

Chet said, "One thing, Charlie. All you have to do is come to Stinson Beach one day around 6 or 7 p.m. and sign all major invoices. That is how the account is set up."

"I don't mind. All I want is my salary for driving over there every day."

Chet said in a joking manner, "I'll believe it for a fee."

I seriously replied, "That's what I am charging: a fee."

We looked at each other and talked to each other with our eyes, allowing them to say what we never would aloud. My eyes said, "I want the same thing from Standard Oil that you want." His eyes said, "A nigger isn't supposed to make this type of money."

We ordered more cocktails and talked. I found out a few things. One was that Standard Oil wanted to keep me from the press. Chet knew I knew how to play the press. One thing Standard Oil didn't want was a scandal. They knew I wanted to make money and they knew that as long as money changed hands, I would only do what I had agreed to do.

In the construction industry, most things were done on a

man's word regardless of whether the businessmen involved loved or hated each other. A handshake and a promise to pay on that handshake constituted a deal. That was why I got along with humanity as a whole; I did what I said I would.

When we looked up at the clock, it was 11:30 p.m.. I said, "Look Chet, I'll see you tomorrow evening around 6:30 p.m.."

# History 9

# "Children"

I drove home while trying to think about our conversation. I didn't make much progress because I have always had a problem explaining bullshit. I went home, took a shower, went to bed and slept like a log. The next morning, my children were all over me asking me questions.

"What are you doing to make all that money?" Dee Dee asked.

I replied, "I go to the beach everyday and bury some money. I water it and the sun shines on it really brightly. Now we have little money trees growing and we have to take care of them to make sure they grow up to be big strong trees."

All of my girls laughed and said, "That's not true, Charlie!"

I then made up other stories about how I made my money. They believed some of the stories; other ones had them stumped. But we had fun and that was all that mattered.

When the girls were done interrogating me, Ann asked, "Would you like to get up, your highness, or shall I serve you in bed?"

I answered, "My beautiful queen can do whatever suits her fancy." She brought the food to the bed. The children and I ate it. More accurately, the children ate it. I left home around 10 a.m.. I looked in the trunk of my car and found I had about seven or eight grams of cocaine left, so I decided to go to Stinson Beach that afternoon and mess around with Fran, Black and Mae. I went to my office and took care of other things. It was surprising how few problems I had when I had money. I went shopping for myself, bought a couple of suits and other stuff and passed the time. It was 4:30 p.m. when I drove to Stinson Beach. I arrived around 6:30.

As I pulled into the driveway leading toward the parking lot, I saw Fran and Mae walking in my direction. I got out of my car and walked in the office. Claudia had a stack of papers for me to sign. I didn't talk to anyone. I wanted to give the impression I was pissed off. When I finished, I went out and found a note on my windshield that read, "Charlie baby, we are up at Mae's house, come by! - Fran."

I drove up to Mae's and had a ball. She, Fran and Black fixed dinner and we danced, drank wine, smoked weed, snorted coke and just hung out. As much as I wanted to go to bed with all three of them, I acted as if sex didn't matter to me. I thought to myself, *"If I go to bed with one of these whores, she will have to ask me to."*

I liked to go on ego trips with women concerning who was going to give in first. I knew that they were trying to figure out why everyone else wanted to go to bed with them and why I ignored them when they made themselves available to me. What they didn't know about me was that I had prostitutes who gave me money and everything pretty didn't bother me. I knew as long as she laid down first, she got up last. I liked to be nice to women without any ulterior motives. I always felt that in most cases women thought that if they had intercourse with a man, then the man was in debt.

Most men were in debt if they didn't know how to satisfy a woman. However, I charged if a woman climaxed and I didn't; I felt that was fair. They continued to play and joke with me. They started playing with each other as they had the last time we were all together.

Once that happened I said, "I got something to do."

Mae stood up and asked, "Don't you like any of us?"

I replied, "Of course. I like all three of you, but not well enough to go to bed with. I don't hop in bed just to be hopping."

Black said, "You ain't that important!"

I replied, "I know that and neither are you," and laughed. "By the way, do you want some more coke?"

Fran asked, "Are you mad with us?"

I said, "No, I am just not into sex this week."

I left them some coke and left. I was not afraid to acknowledge that I wanted to have sex with them, but I wanted to play with their heads, which I did. I knew I could have any of the three I wanted.

I began to think that money was changing me. I laughed as I drove back to San Francisco. I thought, *"If it's the money, then I must have been rich all my life because I do this when I am broke."* I went for a drive to think about some of the things that were taking place. I thought that maybe I should call my other partner, Leroy Cannon. I called and he was home. I told him I was coming by his house the following morning and that I wanted to talk to him.

He said, "Fine. I want to talk to you also."

It was the thirteenth day of my newfound success. I drove by Munich Street that morning. Leroy was a middle-class attorney for the City and County of San Francisco. He was also my partner in the trucking business.

When I first got into trucking, he did all the research on the various permits, licenses, insurance and whatever I needed to get into the business. He was a lifesaver because he had me up and running in two weeks flat.

Leroy and I had met, accidentally, one night at a party. A friend of mine knew him. I had stopped by to pick up a lady friend. When I rang the doorbell, my friend, Bradley, opened the door and heartily shook my hand.

I knew Bradley from my younger days in Hunters Point. He was a little older than me and always tried to look out for me. In

101

fact, I owed my success in the trucking business to him. One hot Saturday morning, Bradley introduced me to Soul Transportation, an organization composed of all black truckers in the Bay Area. Through Soul Transportation I learned about the discrimination that black truckers faced at the hands of Chet Smith and Ralph Rogers. I also learned that because of the discrimination they faced, none of the black trucking companies was very large. I saw an opportunity to be the biggest black trucker and jumped on it. After my first Soul Transportation meeting, I bought three dump trucks and hired drivers within two weeks. A few weeks later, I was protesting in front of BART construction, which led to work for all the black truckers and made me, along with Chet and Ralph the big three trucking company owners in the Bay Area.

While Bradley and I exchanged greetings, Leroy walked up to me and said, "I have heard lots of talk about you."

At that point, Bradley introduced us. All I wanted was to pick up this lady and leave, but Leroy pulled me in the house and started a long conversation about business. However, before I left, he told me that I needed political muscle and he could give it to me. I listened and left as soon as I could. I gave Leroy my home phone number and stayed over at my lady friend's house.

When I came home the next day, Ann was already at her mother's house, but had left me a note saying that Leroy had made a pest of himself. When I returned his call, he said he wanted to have lunch with me. I agreed and a few days later we had lunch together. I kept in contact with him because I knew that being linked to a lawyer with City connections could only be an asset.

I pulled up in front of Leroy's house around 11 a.m. He was standing in front of his garage. I pressed the "unlock" button for the passenger side door.

Leroy opened the door, got in and all in one blast said, "Let's go have a drink. What is going on between you and Standard Oil? Are our personal trucks working over there? Are the drivers over there? Oh yeah, I need some money."

"Okay," I said, "Hold on Bra'. For starters, I'll give you $10,000 tomorrow morning if that will make you happy," I replied. I started the car and drove to Mission Street a few blocks away, went into the nearest bar, got a booth and a couple drinks. We talked for hours. Finally, by the time Leroy was almost drunk, I had talked to him about everything. The entire time I was on the job, we just talked on the phone about payroll and made small talk. This was the first time I had seen Leroy in about fourteen days, although it seemed as if I had not seen Leroy in a year - so much had transpired in just a few days. Leroy expressed his concern. He said, "Those assholes at Standard Oil can have something done to you."

I then told Leroy, "I am not afraid of that."

He said, "If I were you, I would be." Immediately after those words left his mouth, my intuition told me that he knew something I didn't. I then asked, "Hey, do you know something I don't?" He said, "No, but I know their type."

"Well Leroy," I said, "If one of those assholes fucks around, I will show each and every one of them a trick or two. I am not the nigga who understands accidents. I have a couple of friends that I am going to pay $30,000. If anyone in my family has an 'accident' and those assholes didn't have anything to do with it, I won't have anything to do with their 'accident' either. I have enough money to keep half and give the other half away for protection. I know they have a world of money, but my friends don't need anything but the big wheels' addresses. You would be surprised at what a few thousand dollars can buy!"

The day passed. I drove to Stinson Beach and took Leroy with me. I went into the office and signed all the daily work. I felt that it was still important to act like I was pissed off at the world; I shut out the world with a distant stare and scowl. Without making eye contact, I stuck out my hand while one of the clerks handed me another stack of papers to sign. I only waved at Chet and Adell and went into the nearest empty office. I closed the door behind me and signed everything. I then walked out, told the clerk that I left the signed papers on the desk, left the office, got in my car and drove away.

Leroy started asking me hundreds of questions. I lied to him most of the time, selectively telling him what I wanted him to know. The types of questions he asked told me that he didn't know anything and was only concerned in protecting his investments and possibly making some money off my troubles. After meeting Leroy, I knew one thing for certain: he thought he was going to get something for nothing.

The next day, I made sure that Leroy got the money. My intuition again told me that Leroy knew something I didn't, but it didn't matter at that time. I had given Chet the one hundred grand he needed and he seemed pacified. I spent the next few days paying bills, catching up on other things and going to Stinson Beach every day.

I saw Fran a few times. One day I was leaving the office to go back to San Francisco when Black and Mae walked up to my office and asked for a ride to the city. I agreed to take them. During the drive, I asked if they would like to stop and have a bite at Scoma's at Fisherman's Wharf. They said they were starving, so we stopped at the Wharf. We had a nice time eating and talking. During the meal, they repeatedly asked me whom I liked among them.

I knew better than to say either one of them, so I said, "Fran." Just as I thought, Black and Mae laughed and said, "We knew it." Then they went on to tell me some of the things that Fran had said about me. For instance, Fran told them that she liked me, but I did not give her any action. Mae said, "Why don't we get some blow and get together later?"

I had a prior commitment, so I said, "I have something else to do."

Black and Mae got pissed and said I was self-centered. I

retorted, "I wouldn't mind putting my business off; both of you are very attractive ladies. I don't know why, I have the feeling that men do too much for both of you. Unless both of you want to be with me, I am not going to play games. I ain't no sugar daddy to bitches and that's what I think both of you are! So, before either one of you get it bent, I just want to say I am not anything to play with. I have a lot of women and more if I want, so let's just be friends."

"Okay," Black said. "Well, I guess we can leave, Mae." I laughed and asked, "May I drop you ladies off?" Mae said, "Thanks, but we can walk where we are going from here." I picked up the check, paid the cashier and left without saying goodbye.

"When dealing with a small guy,
five grand could mean food on his table"

# History 10

# "Day Twenty One"

The days continued to pass until day twenty-one finally arrived and the shit hit the fan. I had stayed home on the previous day. I didn't feel well because I had been running my ass ragged for too long. Also, Ann's grandmother was ill in Memphis, Tennessee. I got her a 7 a.m. flight on the following day, day twenty-one. After I dropped off Ann at the airport, I had to go back to the house because I forgot my little brown book. I opened the door, went to the bedroom and picked up my phone book. As I turned to leave, the phone rang.

In my usual manner, I said, "Yes" as I put the receiver to my mouth. I heard, "Hey Charlie, this is Wilbert Weston." He continued, "Say Charlie, I need to talk to you. It is very important."

"Okay," I replied. "Where are you?"

He said, "Over at my mother's."

"Okay, why don't you meet me at Zim's on Van Ness Avenue?"

"Fine. How long?"

"About thirty minutes from now. It is a little after eight."

"Eight thirty. Fine," Wil said.

I left the house, got in my car and drove straight to Zim's. During the drive, I didn't think too much of Wil calling. Wil was a San Francisco policeman who would hit the panic button too quickly. However, we met under strange circumstances and I liked him. One day I was speeding in my Cad and Wil pulled me over to give me a ticket. I pulled over while cursing the cops under my breath.

As soon as Wil approached my car and saw that I was a brother, he said, "Brother, watch your step around these other cops; they'll get you quick as fast as you were going. Now have a good day, Bro'." I sat stunned in my car as he quickly walked back to his car and drove off. I later saw him at a club and bought him a drink.

Our conversation that night led to a fruitful friendship. Before I met Wil, I had a driving dislike for black policemen and any type of black law enforcement officer. In my experience, all the white officers I had ever met had sense enough to know what real police work was all about, but Negro police officers didn't have a clue. It was nearly impossible for a black police officer to protect a black person because of a fundamental contradiction: black police officers were just former slaves still trying to protect the owner's life and property. A black police officer could never help a black person because that conflicted with his or her duty as an officer, which was to protect the interests of whites. Regardless of my feelings about black police officers, I always knew that law enforcement was a necessary component of our society. However, I never could figure out how black police officers could get around that fundamental contradiction they lived day in and day out.

As I pulled into the Zim's parking lot, I had the strange feeling that I was being watched. All my antennas went up and I became leery. I began to turn around and leave, but I changed my mind and walked inside. As soon as I entered, I looked all around the place. I felt something that I couldn't put my finger on. I spotted Wil in a booth.

I stopped short of the booth and said, "I don't sit in booths. They make my back ache."

Wil got up and walked over to where I was standing.

We embraced each other with our usual greetings and asked

about each other's family. We sat at the counter and as Wil picked up a menu I stood up quickly and said, "Let's go. I forgot something; I think I left my front door open."

Wil followed me out the front door. As I walked around to the back, Wil asked, "Do you want me to ride with you?"

I replied, "That's fine with me."

He said, "Just a minute."

He went back inside to pay for a glass of milk he drank. He ran in and right out and jumped in the car. I went down to Broadway and started toward the freeway as fast as I could, just barely making a few stoplights.

Wil asked, "What is wrong?" I said, "I don't know; for some reason I felt I was closed in at that place!" Wil laughed and said, "That's why I called you. There is a twenty-four-hour tail on you. I heard some intelligence officers talking about you the other day and you are top secret. All I want to know is what the fuck are you doing?" I replied, "I don't know."

Wil said, "Man, are you hot!" "I think I know what all the fuss is about, but I am not sure. Wil, what did you hear exactly?"

"Well the other day, I was taking a shit and I couldn't see who was around me, but I recognized the voices. One of them was a guy we call the Gestapo! He works directly for Jeremiah Taylor, the guy who invented the TAC squad."

"Well, what did they say?" "Just calm down. I am going to tell you. The police have been trying to break in to your house for a month. They were 'complaining' and Capt. Taylor told them that he was exploring ways to make the break-in appear to be a robbery if necessary. He also said if necessary to scare your wife, slap her around and make it look like you are a drug dealer."

I asked, "What do they want?" "I don't know," Wil replied. "They finished taking a leak and walked out."

"Well, first of all how do you know for sure that they were talking about me?" "Oh, that's what I forgot; while they were taking a piss, one of them laid this down." Wil stuck his hand in his inside coat pocket and pulled out an envelope. I pulled over to the curb and parked so I could look at this shit.

"Wil," I said, "didn't they look for this folder?" "Man, did they! They turned the place upside down looking for it. They didn't know I was in the restroom and there was no way to tie it to me because when I picked it up, I put it in my trashcan and took it downstairs. I removed it at lunchtime. However, when I returned from lunch, Taylor was in the restroom looking for the file. I was called down to the chief's office and asked how well I knew you. One of the officers, Shan, said I wasn't in at the time the folder was lost, so he knew I couldn't have seen the folder. Then I asked, 'What are you talking about?' They said, 'Well, forget it. We lost some papers, I am sure they will turn up.'"

While Wil was talking, I read the folder. I said, "This is a surveillance worksheet on a day-by-day schedule. Very interesting! Well Wilbert, what do I do after this?"

"Well Charlie, I can't let you keep this shit. They would trace it right back to me." "All this shit is about Standard Oil and me. This has nothing to do with me breaking the law!"

"I know," Wil said, "but they are pissed at you because of some shit that occurred. What were you doing with some drugs on the job?"

"What drugs?"

"The drugs you were selling."

"I was not selling drugs. I bought… Hey wait a minute! I see the bullshit now."

I then briefly told Wil what had occurred, focusing on the prostitutes and drugs, how everything was paid for, how the motel owner loaned them the money and how the drugs came into play.

I pulled away from the curb and proceeded to the freeway.

"We will pick your car up later. Is that okay?" I asked. Wil agreed.

As I drove around, I asked, "Well, what do you think I ought to do, Wil?" Wil replied, "I don't really know, but I do know one thing: this is a lot of bullshit. Standard Oil is using the police department for their personal vendetta."

"I know. Since they want to fuck around, I am going to give them something to do." "What, Charlie?" Wil asked. "Well, I am still running things over at Stinson Beach."

"Charlie, just let me say I sure would like to be with you. I don't like police work anymore." "Why?" I asked.

"There is no room for advancement for a black policeman. I have got to get out of the department. The whites dislike all black officers and the black officers don't have any heart. It's a mess. To be truthful, Charlie, America is tired of blacks period. Maybe they should do us the way Hitler did the Jews and we would either stand together or perish. We keep begging them for freedom and they keep starting wars with other countries and putting our black asses on the frontline. After the war is over, we come back only to fight them over a job. I can't be loyal to a police department and this country; it's too much to handle. They keep telling us that things are going to change, but they know, I know and all wise men know that children of ex-slaves don't stand a chance without land or monetary power. Blacks in America need a foreign country to loan us some money so we can buy some equity in America."

I said, "So much for foreign aid, but I am in a war with Standard Oil. They have hired the San Francisco Police Department to help them and all I have is you. I know that this is no time to apply for foreign aid."

We just drove around in circles. I finally asked, "Do you want to go to Stinson Beach with me today?" "I don't care! First, let's stop, get my car and park it somewhere else."

"Okay. We have to pass it on the way to the Golden Gate Bridge."

I turned and started in that direction. It was about 9:45 a.m.

on a beautiful day with light traffic; it was a pleasant day to drive through the rolling hills of Marin.

Flowers bloomed all year in California and the grass was always green. Some of the richest people in the world had homes in Marin County. No matter how many times I drove to Stinson Beach, I always enjoyed the scenery.

Wil and I talked about different things as we curved up and down the hairpin turns and rounded the last turn overlooking the small quiet town that Standard Oil had turned into an equipment ranch. I reflected that the town had shaped up from the last time I had seen it. Wil and I continued down the slope and into the parking lot. As I got out of my car and walked into the office, everyone's noticeably quiet demeanor seemed to spell trouble. I walked into Dan's office. Chet, Stan, Dan and two other men I had never seen before were sitting around Dan's desk with various receipts all over the desk.

I said, "Good morning." Everyone spoke. After the pleasantries were exchanged, the other two gentlemen stood up and introduced themselves as Mr. Petes and Mr. Buchanan, auditors for Standard Oil. I said, "Pleased to meet both of you. This is Mr. Weston, a business associate of mine."

Mr. Buchanan said, "My, my. What a mess." I said, "You should have seen the beach when I arrived." "I'll bet it was," he replied. I went outside and got another chair so Wil and I would each have one. Both of us sat down.

Mr. Buchanan said, "Mr. Walker, on behalf of Standard Oil and Industrial Railway, we have paid out some $500,000 and before we make any further payments, we would like an accounting."

"Chet," I said, "since we received the last payment, approximately how much is the tab?" "I'm not sure, but it is in the neighborhood of $450,000 give or take a little."

"Are you saying that we have to wait until you go through all this mess and set up books before Standard Oil will give us any more money?" I asked Mr. Buchanan incredulously.

"I am afraid so," Mr. Buchanan said.

"Well, Mr. Buchanan, let me be the first to inform you that I am not paying another bill and I am going to stop payment on all the money I have paid. From the last progress payment, I think I have in excess of $200,000 and I will remove my equipment from the job and then see how Standard Oil talks. There is no sense in us talking any further; I understand the rules of the game now. Good day, gentlemen." Wil and I walked to my car. I cranked it up and drove away.

"I have to go to the main office on Bush Street in San Francisco," I said to Wil. Wil asked, "For what?" I replied, "I don't know! I'll play it by ear. I know that pervert, Tennat, is behind this bullshit."

Wil said, "Isn't he the head of Standard Oil on the West Coast? Oh, I didn't tell you, Tennat is involved in some big project with San Francisco city churches. This thing is starting to make sense. Capt. Taylor is a friend of Tennat's; so he is doing Tennat a favor. By the way, Taylor is ruthless! There ain't no telling how much money will change hands. Just think, if Standard Oil can beat you out of your share and give Taylor fifty grand or whatever, Standard Oil will make more money even though you cleaned up the oil and kept the lid on the job."

"Well, I have about $300,000, but I have to pay some of my tabs to small businesses. When dealing with a small guy, five grand could mean food on his table. You don't take food off a man's table or you'll have really bad luck!"

I drove like a bat out of hell. It was around 1:30 p.m. when I got out of my car in the parking lot next to Standard Oil. I walked into their main building, looked at the directory just to be sure the eighteenth floor housed the executive offices. I got in the elevator.

"Eighteen please."

I smelled a stale odor coming from the old building as the elevator bolted up non-stop. Wil and I were the only ones in the ele-

vator at the time, excluding the operator. As we came to an abrupt
stop, the door slid open smoothly. When we stepped out of the elevator, the first person I saw was one of the asses I had seen in the
motel a few days earlier. He tried to run away. I said, "Just a
moment." He stopped, looked at Wil and said, "May I help you gentlemen?" I didn't allow Wil an opportunity to say anything. I started the conversation politely because other people were around us.
We were outside of crowded offices housing secretaries, managers,
vice presidents and all types of Standard Oil big wheels. I planned
to remain cool if this asshole did everything I wanted. I walked up
very close to his face and looked at the little spot where, if God were
going to give us three eyes, the third eye would have been placed. I
felt as though I could see his brain or into the next room. His mouth
went into motion.

"Is there a problem, Mr. Walker?"

"Oh, there is no problem. Where is Tennat?"

Clearing his throat he said, " He is in a very important meeting at this time." "Well, will you go and tell him one of his niggas
has arrived directly from the Stinson Beach Plantation?"

"Mr. Walker, I wish you wouldn't talk like that." "I did not
come here to satisfy your wishes or talk to you. Now if you don't
mind, would you please inform Mr. Tennat that it is imperative that I
speak to him?" "Well Mr. Walker, I can try and get you an appointment."

I couldn't stand this jellyfish. He was making me sick.
"Shut up, you little son-of-a-bitch. Weren't you one of the bastards
running around the motel the other night with Tennat? The way I
look at it, if I can do you a favor and get all of you some…"

Tennat came running out of the office. "Charlie, just a
minute, just a minute. Let's go to the conference room." "We can
go, but we don't need this little private of yours."

"Now, now, Mr. Walker. Let's not resort to name-calling!
This way please." He then addressed his little private saying, "It's
okay. You can just go, Fred. I'll be all right."

I added, "If he ain't all right, you ain't no help 'cause I'll beat your ass if I ever see it again." "Right this way, Mr. Walker," Tennat said. We walked into a large plush conference room. It appeared to be a room where the board of directors might meet; it was very elegant. I sat in one of the nice, dark mahogany chairs. Tennat sat across from me.

"Well Charlie, we must have audits at the end of all jobs."

"I understand all that, but what you are overlooking is that I have outstanding debts that can't wait until they set up books. Besides, it is costing around $5,000 an hour to operate. However, I am going to cut back on one shift starting tomorrow and it should take two or three days to complete the transition."

"Yes," Tennat said. I could see that Tennat was stalling. However, I knew I couldn't just pull all plugs because I didn't know what Chet had done in my absence. So, I also played a game. "I will admit, Mr. Tennat, that things have been run a little loosely. I guess I acted a little hastily, but you must understand that Mr. Buchanan and Dan don't have your tact. By the way, Mr. Tennat, I have sent everybody a partial payment. However, since it will be at least two weeks before I get another payment from you, I would like to pay Walker Trucking, a company owned by my partners and myself; that will really take care of a lot of things. I think that would be reasonable."

"Approximately how much is it, Charlie?"

"I am not sure - about twenty-eight thousand."

Tennat said, "Oh that won't be a problem. However, after that payment, you will have to wait until we finish our audit."

"No problem!" I replied. "Okay, if you will go back over to the job, I'll call Bob of Industrial Railway or Dan Wakeman and tell them to take care of it."

"Thank you, Mr. Tennat. By the way, Mr. Tennat, I lost my stupid temper a few minutes ago out in the hall." "Ah, Charlie, don't let it bother you; you're a good boy anyway." "Thank you, Mr. Tennat."

We shook hands and I calmly walked to the elevator. I noticed as I was leaving that there were two security guards on the floor. As I passed one of them, I said, "Good afternoon, officer." He returned the greetings. The elevator arrived. Wil and I got in and the elevator operator knew to take us straight to the street floor. I never opened my mouth to Wil or the elevator operator, but the next sound I heard was, "Street floor." We stepped out walking at a fast pace. I gave the parking lot attendant my ticket and a $5 bill. It was 2:35 and the afternoon commute hadn't begun yet, so it only took about three minutes before the car was in front of me. I still had not said a word to Wil. We got in the car and Wil pulled out a handkerchief to remove the perspiration from his brow. "Man, you are something else; I have never seen anything like that. I just knew that man was not going to spend another dime. I would have bet my right arm." "And you would be walking around here with one arm for the rest of your life. I understand that a one-armed man's biggest problem is learning how to wipe his ass." We both laughed.

I said to Wil, "Can I tell you something?" Wil said, "Of course!" "I love the game." "What game?" Wil asked. "When all odds are against me, it looks like I haven't got a chance and by all laws I can't win. Wil, it ain't no fun if whites just give us something. That ain't the way they got it and if they just gave all blacks in this country a million dollars today, in one week all car lots would be empty. In two weeks most of them would have been in a wreck and after all the lawsuits were settled, all cars were repaired and all the crap games were over, I would be generous if I said seventy-five percent of the money would be back in the hands of the powers-that-be. We would be right back where we started. No one would think to put other people to work and build something so that their grandchildren would be able to say, 'Good God. All of this is mine and grandpa built it for me. Now it's up to me to take care of it so our family will always be able to say, 'What is this thing they call welfare?'"

Around this time, we were crossing the Golden Gate Bridge.

Traffic was moderate and we made good time. When we arrived at the job, I knew someone might start some bullshit. However, I was surprised. All Dan said was, "How do you charge this?" I said, "All you have to do is make up the truck tags like we did for the ladies of the evening."

"Oh, all right. By the way, Charlie, if I told you my daughter was getting ready to start college and doesn't have a car, what would you say?" I replied, "I would ask, 'What is the most you can make this check for, Dan?'"

"We were instructed not to give you over thirty-three grand." "Okay, make it up and I'll drive to a late Wells Fargo Bank, deposit most of the money and when Wil and I return we will see what can be done about that. By the way, Dan, I want you to make up a lot of those truck tags. The only difference is this time they are not for drugs and pussy." We laughed.

Dan said, "Charlie, I like the way you put things!" "Thank you." He handed me the check after he wrote the amount and told me, "Take this piece of paper with you and give it to the manager. Everything will be all right after that." "I know. Thank you, Dan."

I took the check and drove as fast as I could to the bank. As a black person walking into a bank in the suburbs, all eyes were on me. Wil looked more like a stick-up artist than a cop. Surely I looked like I was up to no good in the eyes of a square white person. When the teller asked, "May I help you?" I was an arm away. I lowered my voice and said, "Yes, let me talk to the manager," using my coldest eyes. She instantly got nervous, stood up and walked to his desk in the rear. He looked up, saw Wil and me and said a couple of words to which she shook her head. He got up, followed her and for a second, it seemed like everyone put their finger on the "hurry-up-and-come-police" button. The teller stepped aside in the direction of her desk. The manager alone was in front of me. "Yes, may I help you gentlemen?" he asked. I smiled and said, "Why not? I am Mr. Walker, president of Walker Trucking and this is Mr. Weston, my associate."

I stuck my hand in my coat pocket, pulled out the envelope and handed it to the manager. His instructions were to call some man; I didn't read the paper. However, whoever's name was on the envelope woke up the manager right away. "Oh, step this way gentlemen." He practically ran back to his desk and pulled up another chair for both of us. I winked at Wil. Everyone in the bank looked in amazement as if to say, "Who in the fuck are they?" The manager made a call and talked to someone. While he was talking, he scanned my face while saying, "Yes. Yes he is. Okay, okay. Yes sir. Yes sir, I am sure sir. Thank you very much. Yes sir!" He hung up the phone, looked up at me and said, "Mr. Walker, I am sure you are, but do you have any identification?" "Sure," I replied. "Wil, show him yours also." Wil pulled his coat back and everybody in the bank began to shake. He showed his badge and identification in the small police wallet. His shoulder holster and gun showed prominently.

"I am Mr. Dean or did I already introduce myself?" "No, but I can understand why," I said and smiled. I was sure both of us knew what I meant. He leaned back in his chair to relax and said, "Well, you are the company cleaning up our little town?" "Yes we are," I said as I smiled again. "You don't want this in cash, or do you?"

"Well, I want about seventy-five hundred in cash. As for the rest, just make me a cashier's check for it." It was done. We left and I laughed and laughed as we drove out of the parking lot. I found the nearest phone booth, stopped and called Dan at the office and told him, "Okay Dan, thank you. Everything is okay. I am going to San Francisco. I am going to call you and at that time have someone bring you and drop you off on California and Van Ness Avenue and either Wil or I will pick you up." Dan said, "Fine. I have someone who can bring me."

"Okay," I said, "talk to you in a few." I hung up and drove to Auto Row in San Francisco, which also happened to be on Van Ness Avenue. I went into Hughson Ford and found a new Fairlane demo model. It was $4163 including tax and license. I hardly opened my mouth. I just told the first salesman I saw what I was looking for and we found it. I went inside his office. He began to make out the papers and I didn't know whose name should be on the papers, so I called Dan and told him to come. The salesman took us around the corner and bought us a drink. We bullshitted for an hour, while Wil kept walking out and checking for Dan. Finally he arrived. We went back to the dealer and finalized the deal. I gave Dan a couple hundred dollars in cash and said, "We are friends." He said, "I understand."

Wil and I left. It was about 6 p.m.. I was on an emotional merry-go-round. I was in the game I loved so much. Everything I did that entire day gave me a high. I was aroused to the fullest extent. No one could imagine how I felt at that moment. When I left the car dealer, I knew I was in a position to play because I had just bought my way into the party with the guy who signed the checks!

"Well," Wil said, "I have seen everything."

"No one knows you are a policeman except the man in the bank; so really no one knows and you were an eyewitness to everything."

"Charlie, you love this. I have never seen you so happy."

"I know. This is all I like. I don't care for any kind of sports. Every black person I have ever met that likes sports is very disloyal. I am sure there are some exceptions, but I have never met them. However, I have to go to the house and take Ann and my children some money. I like seeing them happy and being able to afford everything the children need for a good education. I was never on welfare. My mother and father were not on welfare and there are no streetwalkers in our family."

"If anyone told me how you handle things, I would not have believed it," Wil said. "You are a teacher to black men in business. I know that all I learned in college is great for the system, but I have to be wise enough to make it work for me. I can understand why blacks meet extraordinary obstacles to get into mainstream action.

Real business is not like anything you learn in school. Wow! And to think I went to M.I.T. and wasted all that time. Total bullshit."

We pulled into my driveway. Yolanda was looking out the window. I found the greatest pleasure in parenting was to come home to my children who were glad to see me after a day's work. I had nothing at home but girls. They jumped all over me and I loved for them to do it. Whenever I came home and everyone was there, we would wrestle all over the bed. One day, I broke the window while playing and boy, did Ann get mad!

I took the cashier's check out, handed it to Ann, told her to pay our bills and to save about twenty-five grand. I also gave her a grand in cash and told her I had to go to a meeting.

I shaved, changed clothes, gave Wil $3,000 and kept the rest for miscellaneous expenses.

Wil and I hung out. News about the oil spill was all over the Bay Area and it was common knowledge among most black people that I was running things. People had heard all kinds of stories. We went to a club in Oakland and a guy walked up to me and asked, "Are you the one that was driving the ship and ran into another ship in the bay?" I said, "What?" He did not wait for me to say another word before he said, "Nigga, can't you see?"

The situation was funny and Wil and I couldn't stop laughing.The guy kept talking, "White folks let you drive and you ran into another ship - all that water and you found you a ship to run into." Wil just walked away. There was nothing I could have told the guy. I was given a chance to drive a ship and had fucked it up for the rest of the black people in America, as if black people couldn't make mistakes. All black people who were involved in a different occupation than the masses needed to keep a genie with them so that when they got ready to fuck up, it would step in and make things right.

Soon after, we left that club. Wil and I were on the prowl. We got some snow from a mutual friend and proceeded to prowl until we came upon a prize catch - that night it was none other than

Joyce and a friend of hers. We bullshitted for a while, had a few drinks, dropped them off at home and went back to San Francisco. I dropped Wil off at his car and I went by one of my sports' places where I ended up spending the night.

The following morning, Peggie wanted to serve me breakfast in bed, but I didn't want it. I told her I was going downtown to buy some clothes. She wanted to go, so I took her. We spent money and ate all that day. I bought my wife and the girls some things. I had all of them sent home gift-wrapped. Five o'clock came quickly and I had to go to Stinson Beach; Peggie and I went together. All she could talk about was all the stuff I had bought her. That's when I told her that I wanted her to be my woman for a little while. She said it was good enough for her. I told her I was going to put my arsenal at her house because she was the only woman I had, other than Ann, and I wanted her to be very close to me.

She said, "All I want to do is to be close to you. I'll kill for you or do anything you want. Just let me be one of your women." I told her she had to commit herself to me body and soul. She said, "Give me something to do and see how well I'll do it." I was putting a plan together in my mind and I knew I had to be ready for whatever anyone started.

I was going to pick up my sawed-off shotgun. I also was going to see my friend to get five hand grenades. I knew I had to put some protection on my girls and Ann.

I knew Standard Oil would stoop to anything to get what it wanted - my integrity, and my money. However, I made up my mind that if anything happened to my children or wife, Standard Oil was "accidentally" going to have a big accident.

"The house was packed with love
so thick that I could have cut it with a knife"

# History 11

# "At The Hippo"

I drove to Stinson Beach. The drive over was as beautiful as usual. We had finally made a significant-sized cut through the oil, and sparkling water could be seen reflecting lights from the town surrounded by a thick mass that simply absorbed light. I walked into the office with the same attitude.

Dan walked over and said, "I will meet you at the Hippo on Van Ness Avenue around 9:30 tonight."

I signed some papers and left. I took Peggie home and told her I would be back after the meeting with Dan. I also had to stop and see about some hardware because I was expecting a few problems that I couldn't quite put my finger on. I did not know where or when they might come, but I knew Chet was aware that I had at least $150,000. I knew he also knew that I did not have it in a bank. I knew policemen were involved. Additionally, I knew from some of the things Wil had said that they were not acting in an official capacity. All this meant that someone was going to move on me and I wasn't going to just sit around and let it happen. The worst part was that I was black; the police and Standard Oil were white. Some of the stories Wil told me when he worked in intelligence were down right terrible.

If big businessmen didn't want to pay a big bill to a small

firm, they would get someone in intelligence to plant drugs in the business or on someone, making sure that it would not look suspicious. Then they would have a patrol car make a routine stop of that person and they would have his ass. Wil told me that was the type of thing they were going to do to me. So I knew, as Wil had told me, once you got in the law enforcement's scope, they wouldn't stop until they had your ass, even if they had to frame you. Wil told me how they broke into people's businesses and did whatever they wanted. It was kind of frightening, but I liked the intrigue. I couldn't get out; I was too far in. Like or dislike, I really had no choice but to deal with Standard Oil.

I knew the situation demanded that I contact my best friend. Everyone called him J.H., but I called him Jerry. Other people couldn't call him Jerry, but Jerry was closer to me than anyone except my mother; we would do anything for each other. Jerry could be cold if he had to be and not give a second thought to his actions.

I had called him several times, but for him to stop what he was doing I knew I would have to show my face and tell his woman in person. He and I had a signal. Whenever one of us had to see the other, we had to go to the other's house and say, "Come see about your child." After that point, whatever was going on had to stop.

I went by his place and said to one of his women, "Tell Jerry to come see about his child at the Hippo on Van Ness Avenue between 9:30 and 10:30, or call the house."

That only meant that if he missed me at the Hippo, he should call my mother's and we would connect. I left my message, went to the Hippo on Van Ness Avenue and looked around. I drove downtown and parked my car because I didn't plan on being a sitting duck in the parking lot later that night. I then caught a cab and returned. I arrived at 9:20 sharp. The cab let me out in the parking lot and I walked inside. Dan had not arrived, but at 9:30 sharp he walked through the door. We spotted each other around the same time. He walked over and sat down.

"Dan, how did your daughter like her car?" I asked.

"Fine. She loves it. She asked me where I got it from and I told her that her uncle Charlie gave it to her. Now all she wants to do is see her Uncle Charlie and thank him. How can I explain to her that you are her uncle?"

"Tell her somehow the genes got mixed up or your mother picked up the wrong baby and the hospital had a no return policy." We laughed and ordered some food and beer.

Dan started to talk about everything in connection to Standard Oil, including his needs and how he was underpaid. I understood what it meant for Dan to confide in me. I didn't mind because I could leak things back that Standard Oil knew I shouldn't know and all the bigwigs would look at each other, wondering which one of them was a spy. I planned to say something around Chet that he would know I shouldn't know. Dan went on and on, telling me how many times they would forget my name and call me "that nigger," and how funny it was to everybody. Nothing was meaningful until Dan said, "Today around 12:30, Tennat and a couple other men from the main office were over and we had a very big meeting."

I asked, "Was Chet there?" "Oh yes," he said. "If you don't know, Chet is your enemy." I replied, "Yes, I am aware of it, but without him initially, I would not have made a dime. I know enough people today as a result of this job. However, the day I got this job, he was the only game in town."

"Well, I want you to listen carefully because this situation has gotten out of control. Also, I have never seen the two men that were with Tennat. However, they wouldn't play the bullshit secretive game that Tennat loves. Instead, they directly asked some questions about you. Do you know what all this shit is really about?"

"No."

"It's not so much about the money anymore; now they are scared. They don't want anyone to know that they were in the Seadrift Motel having an orgy and using cocaine. The mistake was borrowing that money from the motel manager. Even that wasn't too bad because everybody forgot about it because you were not supposed to know anything about it. Then Tennat told me to have you sign some forged truck tags and no one knew about the twenty-five grand that was sent to you by helicopter. You told Chet it was about twelve grand. He called himself, ratting on you to Tennat. Now you know about the orgy and drugs and they, Tennat at least, wants to kick you off the job. However, everybody is afraid that you will call a press conference and tell all. This whole thing is getting out of hand. I don't know why Tennat doesn't just talk to you. I am sure the two of you could come to an understanding. Charlie, there is one thing you would not believe: Tennat is dangerous and that whole bunch can't be trusted."

"Why do you say that, Dan?" "Well, Charlie, mainly because they are cowards. They will hire someone to do their dirty work, and perhaps do you harm." I acted as if I was surprised and found what Dan was telling me hard to believe. Dan revealed many things about Chet and everyone else. It was at that point that I said, "I am going to show you how grateful I am to you, Dan."

Dan replied, "You are already an 'A' in my book Charlie." "Well Dan, I have some running around to do. I would like for you to drop me off at my car." "No problem."

On the way to my car, Dan told me about a good deal on two car phones. I agreed to purchase them, and have both installed at Motorola in San Mateo. The phones would run about $7,500 including installation. However, in reality, they weren't going to cost us any out-of-pocket money. All I had to do was sign truck tags, better known as weigh bills. I told Dan to fix everything up and I would come over some time later that night and take care of it. All I knew at that moment was I had to put some protection on my ass.

As Dan drove me to my car, I became concerned when I had not heard from Jerry. I got my car and drove back up on Fell Street; I was in luck. As I pulled up, Jerry was walking out. I was supposed to go visit Peggie, but meeting with Jerry was more important than keeping that appointment.

Jerry saw me parking and as I got out of my car he said, "I was just coming to look for you." He walked down the steps and I said, "You drive; I would rather ride with you."

When we got in his car, I said, "Man, do we have lots to talk about." Jerry and I each had a couple of business ventures that were making money. I had my trucking company and the Standard Oil job; Jerry always had whores and various other undertakings. Jerry liked whores and they liked him. However, we both had square wives and children - our private lives for picnics and family gatherings. All men need a family life or they aren't good for anything; we get our strength from our women. In most cases, when I found a man with no wife or children, I chose not do anything with him, mainly because he couldn't be trusted. "By the way, Jerry, head for the Golden Gate Bridge. I have to go to the job." Jerry said, "Good, I have never been there." I began to talk and tell Jerry about all the things that were going on including the police, Tennat, Chet and everything else I could recollect. We also talked about the meeting I had just had with Dan, how Wil fit in and what Wil heard while he was on the toilet taking a crap. We discussed which steps to take, what to do and to whom.

Finally, Jerry started telling me about one of his whores who had a customer that was a lieutenant on the San Francisco police force. He was a freak, but she sort of liked him because one time he told her of a pending raid on one of Jerry's houses. She said the lieutenant talked about everything to her. She also said he told her that if there was anything that she wanted, he would handle it for her. He also was on the take everywhere. I wasn't surprised. I knew a lot of policemen on the take. I made arrangements with Jerry to get the woman to set up a meeting and for her to tell him he could make a nice piece of money. We also planned to call Joe and have some of his friends watch our homes at night.

Joe was a childhood friend of mine. When I was a child, Italians and blacks populated the Bay View and Hunters Point, we all liked each other and ran around together. Their family lives were just like ours except they spoke a different language and were a different color, but color generally means nothing to children. My mother would treat an Italian kid as if he were one of hers, and Italian mothers would do the same by us. My closest friend was an Italian kid, Joe Guido, who everyone called "Little Joe." Little Joe's mother could not speak English, so I picked up Italian in communication with her over kid's stuff. His father worked for the Sunset Scavenger Company driving a garbage truck. I used to call Joe's father Mr. Paisano. When he drank wine that he made in his basement, he would call me "Little Black Sicilian." When he was not drinking, we would call each other Paisano. Although Joe's parents later moved to Silver Terrace, Joe and I remained friends while growing up. Joe and I eventually grew up and went our separate ways. Joe traveled a lot and we saw each other sporadically.

One day, long after my childhood days of running around in Hunters Point, I went to lunch at Bruno's on Mission Street in San Francisco. It was very crowded. About midway down the bar, an older man sat with a lot of people around him drinking a toast to his retirement. All of a sudden, when I looked in that direction, Joe and his father started calling me Little Black Sicilian and laughing. Everyone in the bar got quiet. Joe and his father got up and we walked toward each other. His father spoke in Italian, so I answered him in Italian. We hugged and kissed for ten minutes.

Mr. Guido told everyone in the bar I was also his son and that he had raised me. I walked in with a young lady, but I forgot she was with me. She got mad and stormed out. More people came and everyone ate. Joe and I sat next to his father and I drank wine until I was drunk. At the end of the evening, Joe and I talked about old times and reaffirmed our love for each other. That night he told me he was in charge of Northern California collections for Las

Vegas. He also said that if I ever needed help in any way to call him at the number he gave me. It did not matter what I needed; I could call him. We were brothers. Joe and his friends helped me through my first weeks in the trucking industry. He helped put pressure on Chet and Ralph to hire black truckers while helping me plan my strategy of attack. When I was arrested after my BART demonstration, Joe bailed me out. He and his friends even suggested ways of getting the crucial media attention garnered by the demonstration, which caused the city officials behind BART to force Chet and Ralph to hire black truckers. Ever since that time, I had kept in contact with Joe because he always looked out for my best interests.

After discussing Joe, and what we would ask of him, I planned to make arrangements for Ann and the girls to stay over at her mother's more often. Rudy's house was more secure and Rudy would not hesitate to shoot someone if necessary. Jerry and I understood that in most cases black guys who would get into a mess with drugs would stand around afterwards until someone came and killed them, their family, and friends. The police's standard policy was their "30-30" plan when it came to solving a black murder - thirty feet or thirty seconds, whichever came first.

We finally arrived at Stinson Beach. It took us a little longer because it was foggy and the roads were slick. Most of the night work had stopped, but there still was quite a bit of equipment around and a few people working. It was quite late when we arrived. Dan had already gone to his room at the Seadrift, so we walked up to his room. As we touched Dan's door, the door opened and revealed that Dan had company, a real cutie! Jerry also thought she was quite a dish. I said, "I guess every man has a lady." *"All things aren't pre-dictable,"* I thought. Dan excused himself, came outside and floored me. His lady in the room worked for me and wanted to meet me. Dan introduced her to Jerry and me. Jerry and I started a conversation with her, but she ended up with Jerry and a week later was a whore. Jerry was an amazing man. Every woman he met wanted to be a prostitute for him and they were loyal.

Dan and I talked while I signed many blank truck tags. Dan gave me a check for $11,000 and instructed me to be at a Wells Fargo Bank as soon as one opened so I would not have any problems. I agreed, it always amazed me how white men could call each other and regardless of what one wanted the other to do, there was never any problem getting it done. It was around 2:30 a.m. when I left Dan, and his girl company went with us.

Jerry and the young lady were hugging and kissing as I drove Jerry's car back to the city. We both knew what had to be done. I knew Jerry would do his part. I knew his woman would set up the date with the lieutenant.

I picked up my car and drove home. I glanced at my clock; it was 4:30 a.m.. I parked outside. Most of the time I would pull inside the garage, but if there was a possibility of something going wrong, I didn't want to be in my garage. I walked upstairs and went inside. Ann was a light sleeper. As I entered my bedroom, Ann said, "The police came by here looking for you." "Did they leave a message?" "No. However, they left their card." I was beat, but I thought I would call Wil and ask him if he knew the name on the card. I did, but he was not home. I went to bed and went out like a light. I was awakened by someone ringing the doorbell and banging on the front door. Ann and the children were gone - children in school, Ann out shopping; I had checked the house. I quickly put a piece between the pillows on the couch and a .25 automatic in my robe pocket. I could see if anyone was on the porch, but they couldn't see me. Sure enough, there were two white police officers standing there - I could recognize police officers anywhere in the world. I laughed for a split second remembering when I was in Nigeria; I saw two plain-clothes police arresting a man in the airport, and I thought to myself, *"a plain dick looks the same anywhere in the world."* I approached the front door, stood off to the side and said, "Yes?" "F.B.I.," one of them said. I said, "What can I do for you? I am on the phone!" "Is

Mr. Walker in?" "Yes, I am Mr. Walker." "We would like to talk to you." "May I see your identification please?"

He knew how to do it; he pulled out his wallet and stood back with one arm extended. I said, "Well, what do you want to talk about?" As I said that, I opened the door and stepped outside. I wasn't about to let them in my house, especially since I was alone.

The little cross-eyed one said, "You mind if we step inside?" I said, "Yes, I mind! Only people who are welcome can do that."

At that point the little cross-eyed bastard got smart and said, "Well it doesn't matter; I have been in better places." I shot back, "Well, if you don't have a warrant for my arrest, you are trespassing on private property and I am going to ask you to leave. Don't come back without a warrant."

I backed into the door and slammed it quickly. I realized afterwards that I should have found out what they wanted, but by then it was too late for that. I got dressed, drove downtown to the federal building and went to the F.B.I.'s office. I figured I better find out what they wanted. Well, that didn't work.

The officers I wanted to see were out; "Leave your name, Mr. Walker, and they will get back to you," is what the receptionist said. By that time, it was around 10:15 a.m.. I had the check Dan gave me, so I went to the bank and cashed it with no problems because the manager and I knew each other. After cashing the check, I paid for the telephones and went back to San Francisco. Gene of Tri-City Communications gave me an appointment for Saturday to have the phone installed. I also called Dan to let him know that everything was going along well.

Later that day, Jerry and I met. Val, his whore, had an appointment with some guy and said we couldn't see the lieutenant. I decided to wait because if I couldn't see the lieutenant, the entire arrangement was bullshit. Meanwhile, Jerry and I talked until lunchtime. At that point, I left Jerry knowing that we would get together later.

"I Needed To Prepare Myself
For The Ultimate Kill"

# History 12

# "Police Stopped Me"

After leaving, I decided to grab a bite to eat. I was heading east on Oak Street, a one-way street. While still on Oak Street, I looked in my rearview mirror and saw a car run the red light I barely made. The driver was speeding like a bat out of hell. Though it was a plain car, there were police in it - they put their flashing red light on the dashboard. I didn't know they were after me; I only changed lanes to let them pass. Then they turned on the siren, pulled up close behind me and signaled for me to pull over. I parked beside the curb and got out at the same time as the two police officers. We walked onto the sidewalk.

I politely asked, "What can I do for you gentlemen?"

"My name is Sam," said the officer with a medium build, "and I want you to remember it." I said, "Okay. I have a good memory." He said, "You had better because I got something to tell you and it would pay for you to remember it." "Okay," I said. "Now listen," he said. "Jerry is your partner; he is a pimp! You and Jerry mess with a lot of drugs. Also, you are a partner to San Francisco City attorney Leroy Cannon and you are having a problem with some very important people in this city, such as Standard Oil. Charlie, we are going to piss in your punch." "Thank you, sir," I replied.

"Just to show you a sample of what we are going to do, we

are going to search your car now. The next time we are going to find some drugs. However, all this can be avoided." I asked, "How?" "Simple, just walk away from the Standard Oil job and pay your bill because Standard Oil gave you close to a half-million big ones. You are making our friend look bad."

"I don't know where you got your information, but whatever you say. Is that all?" "Just don't forget, smart nigger."

I immediately drove to Stinson Beach. It was a day of discoveries, but I did not ascertain anything I didn't already know. There was one phenomenon in my life that was unexplainable - nature, God or Allah, as I was more comfortable to reference the Creator, would whisper in my ear to make me aware of danger. However, when I was preoccupied with foolishness, I couldn't hear anything and when that happened I got into trouble; my hearing was bad most of the time.

As I walked through the door entering the office, Chet rose from a desk and walked toward me. He said, "Let me talk to you."

I replied, "Why not?"

I could tell right off when bullshit was in the game. "Let me talk to you," was the signal. I knew I was about to get fucked. We stepped into Shard's office. However, Shard was down on the beach. In fact, Chet and I were the only bosses around. I thought that was a little strange, but I ignored its portent.

"What's really going on Chet?" I asked while I walked into the office and sat down. "Well Charlie, Standard Oil wants to terminate its relationship with you." "No problem," I replied, "but what do they want?" "Well, they want you to take care of your obligation and in return they are willing to pay your commission."

"Chet, before we discuss this any further, let me remind you of a few things."

"Fine," Chet replied.

"First of all Chet, I am mixed up."

"Why is that, Charlie?"

140

"I have the distinct impression at this point that you are my boss."

"No, not at all Charlie." "Well, if you aren't my boss, how in the fuck did you get enough nerve to discuss anything with me? But since you brought this message to me, let me give you a message to deliver to Tennat.

"Start off by telling him that I don't discuss business with my employees because that's what you are. I made you my partner. You don't have my permission to discuss me with Standard Oil. Also, while you are talking to that son-of-a-bitch, I want you to be sure and inform him that I am not afraid of him or those police officers that he called on me."

Chet asked, "What police?"

"He will understand! Also tell him that I said I am not one of those niggas who has rabbit in him. I'll fight back! The next time the police stop me will be considered as a threat on my life and my family's life. I care as much for my family as he cares for his." I walked out of the office, got in my car and drove straight to Standard Oil's main office only to discover that security guards were now stationed in front of the elevators. As I entered the building, one of them walked up to me and said, "May I help you?"

"Yes, you can escort me to Mr. Tennat's office," I replied while I continued to walk directly into an elevator. At that point the elevator operator stepped out of the elevator and the security guard reached for me. As he did, I snatched my arm away, pushed the elevator button and the door immediately began to close. The security guard tried to enter the elevator and I punched him squarely in the mouth. As he backed off to massage his jaw, the door closed and I ascended. I thought I had pressed the nineteenth floor button. When the elevator stopped, I stepped out to discover I was on the eighteenth floor. I walked out anyway and just as I rounded a corner, the first people I saw were Tennat and the bleeding security guard. Tennat hostilely asked, "Mr. Walker, what the hell is the big idea?" I retorted, "First of all, you tell that monkey-suit wearing security guard to keep his hands to himself because the next time he touches me, I am going to break his hand. If either of you think I am bullshitting, just touch me."

"Now, now, Mr. Walker. We don't have to resort to that type of animal behavior." "Fine," I said, "if he keeps his hands to himself, I'll do the same. I am here to talk to you, Tennat." Tennat turned and walked down the hall while saying, "Okay, let's go." I followed him to a conference room and as we entered I said, "I came here for one reason. Look Tennat, I am not afraid of your friends on the police force because I have resolved that if anything happens to anyone in my family 'by accident,' I want you to always keep in mind that you live in Sea Cliff; you have a wife, children and grandchildren.

"To demonstrate that I am not afraid, the next time the police bother me, I am going to notify everyone in your family of your actions. I will also hire some people to form a picket line in front of your home. I am referring to your home in Palm Springs, the one in Orlando, Florida, and your cabin in the mountains near Clear Lake. I am not going to be pushed around by you!"

I immediately turned and walked away. I walked all the way from the eighteenth floor to street level. I hastily walked across the street to where I had parked my car in a red zone. Two tickets lay limp on my windshield. *"So what!"* I thought. I said to myself, *"Well, Charlie, you sure got yourself in a little shit, but it's not so bad since you have money."*

I needed to retreat and just disappear for a few days; regroup. I didn't want to act rashly or overreact. I had to act blasé; I was being jammed.

I knew one thing: I was no competition for Tennat. As I thought about Tennat, I knew there was only one thing that could be done to him: catch him and just blow off his head. That's what I was willing to do if anything happened to my wife or children. Life would not be worth living if something happened to Ann and my children. I could get me some explosives and blow up the

142

Richmond refinery. I needed to prepare myself for the ultimate kill: Tennat and his whole family - if he harmed my family.

Where was I headed? I didn't know; I was just driving. I decided to call Jerry and put him on top of everything. I also resolved to send Ann and the children to Memphis to visit Ann's grandmother. I didn't want them around in case things got nasty. I would head in another direction, take care of some business, then stop by and visit them in Memphis. I knew I had to see my paisanos. It was a standing rule: everyone was entitled to at least one favor.

On a couple of occasions I had to do favors for people I didn't know, but that was just how the game worked. I actually preferred to give favors when I didn't know anyone involved; that way, nothing was personal and it was just another job. I had been loyal to everyone and I was dependable; I never missed. So, I needed a favor now.

I got Jerry on the phone and had a long talk with him. We met later that night to come to some conclusions about my mess with Standard Oil. We went to dinner at a friend's restaurant on Lombard Street in San Francisco. There was no place in the world like La Boucane. Jacques, our friend, met us at the door and hugged both of us; we had not seen him in quite a while. No one could go there without a reservation, but Jacques never required one from us. The funny thing about Jacques was that he was a black man passing for white or French. With his beautiful accent, women loved him. White women just went crazy over him. I would tease him and call him a "call pimp" - the opposite of a call girl. Jacques could speak ten or fifteen foreign languages. People gawked at us when we spoke Italian. Jacques spoke Italian as fluently as an Italian. After hugging us, Jacques said with a thick French accent, "Your highnesses, your table is ready."

It was hard to keep from laughing because when he would say "your highness," he would say it loud enough so half the customers could hear him. All of them would stop eating and stare.

I would try to act modest. Once I went there to eat with my

children and when Jacques said that, all three of my daughters fell out laughing. Pookie fell on the floor and Landi and Dee Dee repeated, "Your highness, your highness," while laughing hysterically. I also had to laugh. Jerry and I sat and Jacques said, "I am going to fix you guys something special." We reclined, talked and drank some wine while Jacques baked us some bread. Whenever I ate with Jacques, my meal would last for four or five hours, but I would enjoy every moment of it.

Words could not express the deliciousness of the food. During dinner, Jerry and I got down to brass tacks. Jerry said, "If you think this asshole might do something to Ann and the children, I will go down to the Standard Oil main building's basement parking lot. When he comes out, I'll kill him and whoever is with him. Or I could be a television repair man and go to his home in Sea Cliff to do whatever I have to."

"Let me say this Jerry, somehow we have got to let that bastard know that what he thinks of niggas doesn't apply in this case." Jerry said, "I would love to blow off this asshole's head. Standard Oil may get one of us, but believe me, if they get me I want you to get even."

"I feel the same way; if they get me I want you to get even. You know Jerry, I have been thinking. I wonder if we can get some dynamite. If so, I will go to Stinson Beach and booby trap a bunch of those big wheels with a trick I learned in the service."

"That sounds like a good idea," Jerry said.

"Oh, did you ever find out what was going on with the lieutenant and Val?" I asked. "Yeah, you won't believe this crap. He's still on the take, but apparently, you are such a big issue with the SFPD that he doesn't want to risk his ass for you. He doesn't think you could possibly have enough money to make it worthwhile to get involved." "Man, this just keeps getting bigger and bigger. Tennat thinks he is going to do all this while I just lay down and take it. I'm definitely getting this asshole."

About this time Jacques brought the food: roasted duck with mandarin oranges, fresh string beans, more fresh bread, rice and freshly baked tomatoes with a cheese topping. "For dessert," he said, "I made chocolate mousse."

Jacques sliced the duck at the table and made quite a scene. Jacques was a first class chef and waiter. He really knew his trade. The food was second-to-none. I smiled when I received the $127 check for dinner for two. In addition, I left a $15 tip, but we thoroughly enjoyed the savory food. Who was it that said, "You get what you pay for?"

After eating, Jerry and I went for a ride and put the final touches on our plan. Jerry and I got along so well because we could trust each other and we would do anything for each other. One time a guy said he was going to do something to me. Jerry ran over him with my car and told me about it the next day, laughing like hell. He said he had just left the hospital visiting the guy he ran over. He told the guy that the next time he said he would do something to me, he would run over his head with the same car.

Jerry had me drop him off downtown. After dropping him off, I went home and found Ann watching television. I joined her and we talked for a while. Finally I got around to telling her that I wanted her to take a trip to Memphis. I made it seem as though I wanted to meet her entire family. She was very happy that she and the kids were going to go see her grandmother. I explained that I would come on the weekend.

Ann immediately got up and packed for herself and the girls. I made the reservations with Delta for a 7:05 a.m. flight. After packing, Ann set the alarm for 4 a.m.. While she finished packing, I drove to the airport and picked up the tickets. I bought four first class round-trip tickets. I returned and at 4:00 a.m. sharp. Ann had the children up and getting ready for their trip. They were jumping around and glad to go. I ordered a limousine to pick them up from the airport in Memphis. I drove them to the airport and made sure they boarded their plane safely. While I was at the airport, I bought tickets to Orlando, Memphis and back to San Francisco. I went back home and made a lot of calls.

I called Jerry to let him know that Ann and the children were gone. I told him where the house keys were and that he could keep the house while we were out of town. I had forgotten that Jerry already had a set of keys to the house. It was early Wednesday morning on day twenty-four and I was not leaving until Saturday. During our conversation, Jerry said, "Read Friday's paper." I replied, "I don't want to read the paper. I am leaving Thursday instead of Saturday."

On Thursday I went to Los Angeles to visit a friend. I took Norma, my little black one with so much class. I checked into the Century Plaza Hotel. Norma and I hung around town until Saturday. Norma went back to San Francisco while I went to Orlando, Florida.

On Sunday morning, day twenty-eight, I had a meeting with Frank and Lileo, two of Joe's friends that were pivotal to my success in the trucking industry, to discuss all the bullshit with Standard Oil. Both of them had big connections with the Teamsters. I went to the meeting not knowing that we would end up talking for five and a half hours. Frank was unhappy because he thought there was a much better way to handle Tennat.

"I wish you would not make plans alone. We don't make moves alone," Frank continued. "I talked to Jerry and Joe this morning. You sure have a mess out there. Why don't you buy another business and back off that construction? You are drawing heat. We can squash that shit with Standard Oil, but you need to keep a low profile. Standard Oil is a powerful outfit. They can cause a lot of trouble."

"I think that's a good idea," Lileo said. I replied "Let me just say, I don't care about anything but my family."

Frank replied, "Oh Charlie, no one is going to bother your family." Frank continued, "I am coming out to California to stay for awhile. By the way Charlie, how long are you going to be out and about?"

"A couple of weeks to a month."

We talked most of the day, rode around and saw the sights. Frank's boat was docked at Key Biscayne. I wanted to see it, but time didn't permit; Frank had to go to New Jersey. I rented a room at the Holiday Inn for the night, made some calls and got a good night's sleep. I did not call Ann; I wanted to surprise everyone.

I left Orlando headed for Memphis and arrived around 10:30 p.m. Sunday night. I caught a cab and went to Ann's grandmother's house. Boy, what a nice person she turned out to be! Ann looked and acted very much like her. I stayed for a week.

I had never gone to a dog race in my life, so Ann's uncle took me across the bridge to Hope, Arkansas, where I had a fun night betting on dogs.

On the third day of my trip, I went on a sightseeing tour of Memphis. I saw Beale Street and enjoyed the charms of Memphis. The highlight of the trip was an old-fashioned southern-style dinner. I never had fried chicken freshly killed from the backyard or cabbage pulled from the garden; everything I ate was either freshly killed or picked out the earth.

Hospitality in Memphis was different than what I had experienced in San Francisco. In Memphis I knew that the most wonderful feeling a human being could experience was being around other people, truly feeling welcome and experiencing genuine honesty.

One thing my children found interesting about Memphis was that everyone had to go to church and there were no exceptions for children.

Later that day, Yolanda ran up to me and said, "Charlie, Charlie, guess what?"

"I can guess," I replied. "All children have to go to church." "Charlie, even if you are sick you have to go to church." "Did you go?" "Yes, Pookie and Dee Dee went too. Pookie went to sleep and got in trouble with the Sunday school teacher, but it was fun. I like going to church with everybody."

After my delicious southern dinner, I went to bed. I thought, "No wonder there are so many children; everyone goes to bed after dinner." The rest of the week was filled with food at the homes of different relatives. Everyone in Memphis had a nickname. Pee Cat was the name of one of Ann's cousins. She was a beauty. Also, most families were close and clannish. Toward the end of my trip, someone asked, "Are you going to church with us tomorrow?" Ann said, "He is leaving at 11:45 tonight," before I could ask what day of the week it was. If the conversation had not taken place, I would have stayed a few more days. I spent the rest of the day at Aunt Thelma's house and everyone came by to say goodbye. The house was packed with love so thick that I could have cut it with a knife.

Fifty people went to the airport with me. I kissed everyone, boarded the plane and fell back in my first-class seat. I instantly went to sleep and in what seemed like seconds I was landing in San Francisco. Early on Sunday morning, thirty-five days after I began my job with Standard Oil, I was home.

When I arrived, Jerry was at the house. We were glad to see each other. We sat around talking most of the day. Jerry told me that he had talked to Frank, Lileo and everyone else. During the conversation, I decided to share an idea with Jerry.

"Jerry, I am going to open a night club for us. I am going to back off of this bullshit for a while." Jerry said, "I don't care what you do. I like what I am doing and I am not going to stop." "Look Jerry, we have to back up and do something different." "Look Charlie, I don't want to do that. I like sportin' ladies and all this madness. I like it! I am not going to run a business. Fuck that. You run the business and I will keep going this way. If something goes wrong, we can fall back on one or the other."

"Okay Jerry, as long as you have my back on this. I'm going

148

to make sure my club is a big hit."

Jerry and I continued to sit around and talk about our plans. We congratulated ourselves on the start of a new business.

# History 13

# "Best Friend Jerry"

$J$erry finally left the house in the wee hours of the morning, but I couldn't go to sleep because my mind was racing with plans for the future. Before I could move forward, I had to settle some things down at Stinson Beach. Once I put aside my ego and looked at the situation somewhat objectively, I knew that I couldn't return to the job. The situation had escalated too far and I didn't know what Tennat would have those white boys do to my family or me. My last encounter with Tennat showed me that Standard Oil's attitude toward me had changed from conniving to openly hostile. Although I desperately wanted to fight for my job, money and pride, my family was too important for me to get sidetracked with Standard Oil's bullshit. I resolved to visit Chet later that day and work out a mutually favorable agreement.

I woke up at 7 a.m. a little surprised that my body only required three hours of sleep. After recovering from the shock of being awake that early, I immediately took a shower and got dressed. I called Chet's house to see if he was there. I luckily caught him right as he was headed out to Stinson Beach. After Adell told him I was on the phone, he instantly picked up.

"Hey, Charlie. What's up?" he asked.

I said, "I need to talk to you right now. Can you wait for me to drive to your place? I'll pick you up and we'll go some place to talk." Chet answered, "Well, I was heading to Standard Oil's main office. Can you meet me there?" I incredulously said, "Are you really asking me to go back there?"

At that moment I knew Chet had already heard of my last friendly discussion with Tennat.

I continued, "Look Chet. I made you my partner and now I need to talk to you. Are you going to wait?" Chet quietly said, "Yes."

I drove straight to his house and picked him up. We agreed to stop at a little café not far from his home to grab a bite to eat and discuss matters. At the café, I ordered a large cup of coffee to keep my energy running high. Chet ordered a donut and coffee. As soon as the food arrived, Chet began to devour his donut; he was apparently hungry.

After eating three-fourths of his donut, Chet finally asked, "So what do you want, Charlie?"

I replied, "Chet, I'm never going back to Stinson Beach or Standard Oil's office. You know the deal; I know you do. I'm through with Standard Oil and all of its madness. I was there for a month and they tried to drive me crazy; I'm done. However, don't think I'm not going to get my money. I'm going to get my fifty percent commission, but I'm going to get it through you. I'm only dealing with you, partner."

Chet said, "Shit, Charlie! I still can't believe things have gone this far."

I knew that asshole was lying because Dan verified that Chet had been double-timing me for a while.

He continued, "Charlie, regardless of what has happened between you and Standard Oil, you are still my partner. We initially agreed on a fifty-fifty cut and you're still going to get it. You can count on it."

The minute he said that I could count on him, I knew that troubles were lying in store for me. Anytime a businessman tried to act like an honest boy scout, I immediately knew that I was going to get screwed hard.

I kept my thoughts to myself and simply said, "Chester, you're not such a bad guy when you don't want to be."

We laughed. Chet ate the last remnants of his breakfast while I finished my coffee. We created a payment schedule where I would pick up my commission every three days from his house. We shook hands and left.

As I drove home, I knew something was wrong. My stomach was in knots and growled loudly; those were the two events that always foreshadowed the drama ahead. I was still pissed at the way things had turned out, but I was at least mildly comforted in knowing I'd never have to deal directly with Standard Oil again.

The day was February 23, 1971. I couldn't help thinking back to the day when all of the drama and turmoil began: January 19. In so few days, my life had changed dramatically. I looked forward to peaceful months ahead and the wonderful day when the beach would finally be cleaned and my contract, hence all connections, with Standard Oil would be officially and permanently over.

When I got home, I looked forward to the hugs and kisses from my girls, all four of them. Only my girls could have dispelled my horrible mood. I opened the door, expecting to hear the shrieks of my girls playing and Ann screaming telling them to be quiet. However, all I heard was silence. I walked up the stairs calling their names, "Ann! Landi! Dee Dee! Pookie?" Dead silence. I sat down on my bed and only then realized that they were still in Memphis. I had gotten so upset I had forgotten that I left them early to take care of some business.

*"Man, you are trippin',"* I said to myself. I then checked the messages and found out that Ann had left me a message reminding me that she and the girls would be home the next day.

I thought, *"Cool. I still have a day to get everything together. I have to hop on this club business."* I called Joe Guido and gave him an update on Standard Oil. I then told him that I wanted to open a club and lay off the trucking business.

He said, "That's good. Standard Oil is getting too crazy. Do you need any help with the club?" I said, "Not now. I still have money coming in from Standard Oil, so I just have to get started. I'll let you know if anything comes up." Joe replied, "Let's hope nothing does." I hung up and decided to call Leroy.

I called and had him research what I needed to legally run a club. He asked a million questions about my job with Standard Oil. I lied, told him everything was fine and promised to bring him some cash. Nothing shut him up quicker than cash.

I then decided to go look at buildings available for rent. I knew that I wanted my club to be big and for that to happen it had to be in the Fillmore District because it was the best "kick-it" spot. I jumped in my Cad and drove around the area to see what was available. I really didn't expect to find anything because most businesses in that area were successful, but I thought it was worth a try. I drove through the area looking closely at the layout of the area, trying to figure out what would be the best location for my club. I drove along the main street looking at what was available. One particular building caught my eye, so I parked and got out. I walked around and saw only one "Space Available" sign in the window of a suite amid the long complex of shops and businesses. From the outside, the suite looked pretty small, but I knew that there was more space hidden inside. A seemingly small space was perfect because it created a cozy and sexy atmosphere that wasn't too cramped.

While I waited for the proprietor to answer my several knocks, I imagined the possibilities: I envisioned that suite remodeled and redecorated. I imagined long lines of people waiting to pay their $5 to get into my joint. The area guaranteed a crowd because it was always full of young shoppers and my only competition would be an old bar that no one really frequented. By the time the owner opened the door and snapped me out of my daydream, I knew that this was the place.

The owner appeared and opened the door. A distinct frown appeared on his face when he got close enough to see that I was black. He opened the door and gruffly asked, "What do you want?" I said, "I'm interested in this place." His frown instantly changed and he said, "Come right in."

I entered and he showed me to a seat. I realized that I was sitting in a closed-down restaurant. I asked him why he shut down. He said, "These kids want something new. I've been here for a long time; it's time for some change."

I thought, *"That's great because I love to shake things up!"* We continued to talk and he gave me the stats on the building. He seemed very eager to sell and I made him an offer he couldn't refuse. We shook hands and he said he would get the paperwork started immediately. After forty minutes, I left the Fillmore District well on my way to owning a nightclub.

I went home, called Jerry and told him about my new place. We talked for a couple of hours about my plans and then he hung up to go visit one of his sports. I tried to plan my next steps, but my body gave out and I fell asleep. I spent the rest of the day alternating between watching television and sleeping.

I was awakened the following morning by my daughters yelling, "Charlie! Charlie! Are you still asleep?" The limousine I ordered for them dropped them off around 10:30 a.m.. The girls ran into my bedroom and jumped on the bed saying, "Wake up! Wake up! We have stuff to show you."

I sat up in bed, though a little groggy, and listened to their stories. They told me about their trip to the zoo and the airplane ride home. While they were talking to me, Ann unpacked everything and fixed them a snack. When she was settled, she told them to go eat their snacks downstairs.

After the girls ran downstairs, Ann asked me what I had been up to while she was still in Memphis. I told her I bought a nightclub. She said, "What?" I repeated more slowly, "I bought a nightclub."

I then told her about my conversation with Jerry and my decision to leave Standard Oil alone. I also told her about the great deal I got on the club. After she heard everything, Ann was relieved to have me home more and not worry about those crazy white boys. I told her that I was now in the planning stage, but still had money coming in from Stinson so she had nothing to worry about. With that, Ann gave a sigh of relief and told me about her trip.

I spent the next few days making plans for the club. I talked to Leroy every day because there were so many technical things to handle. One day he would call about a liquor license, another day he would call me about some new insurance policy I needed. We had to get the necessary permits to remodel and had to hire staff. Every third day I went by Chet's to pick up my check.

The first day I went to pick up my check was a beautiful late February morning. Chet was there to hand it to me and give me a brief update on the job. We shook hands and I deposited the check in my new club account. I only took out enough money to pay for bills, miscellaneous expenses and a little bit of fun. I went home and met with the architect and contractor Leroy hired to remodel the place.

The next two weeks passed by in a blur of meetings with the architect, contractor, interior decorator, newly hired staff and about a million other people. Even though I was busy, I was still home more and my girls noticed.

When Pookie realized that I was staying at home more and wasn't going to the beach, she asked, "Why aren't you out making money, Charlie?"

I said, "I'm still making money. But now I get to do it while being home with you guys more."

She instantly said, "Yeah! I'm glad. I like money, but I like you better." I said, "Good. I like you better too." I was glad to finally be with the girls more. I didn't realize how much I missed them while working at Stinson Beach.

Though the proceeding days were a blur full of club preparations, I distinctly noticed a marked change in Chet. He was home when I picked up my commission three days later. However, Chet wasn't home when I came by to pick up my third check. He left it with Adell and she gave it to me. When I came by three days later, no one was home. Chet simply left a note on the door telling me that the check was in his mailbox. By that time, I already knew what was coming. I called him that night to see what was happening. When Chet picked up I said, "What's going on Chester? Are you trying to pull something?" He replied, "What are you talking about? The check was there. I just had to handle some stuff at the beach." Chet provided an explanation and I let it go. I knew what he was trying to do and I was prepared for it.

As soon as I pulled into Chet's driveway to pick up my fifth check on March 16, he immediately ran out of the house. I could tell by his facial expression that he didn't have my check. So I bluntly asked, "So where's my check?"

Chet said, "Calm down, Charlie. Let's talk about this."

When I heard those words I knew I was in for more bullshit.

Chet said, "Come in, Charlie."

I followed him into his house and we sat down on his couch.

Chet began, "Look, Charlie. Standard Oil wants you to finish paying all the bills you were supposed to with the hundred grand they gave you. Until you resolve that, I can't give you any more money."

I immediately replied, "Don't give me that shit, Chester. You just don't want to give me my money anymore. You're running the job now, but don't forget that I made you my partner. Without me, you wouldn't have any commission."

"I know, I know, Charlie," Chet interrupted. "But you're forgetting that I'm still working for Standard Oil and I don't want to

157

get mixed up in this mess. I just want to do my job and get my money." Only two weeks after we made the deal, Chet was backing out.

"That's fine. But until you give me my commission, Standard Oil won't see a dime of that hundred grand." "But Charlie..." Chet said.

I cut him off and said, "It's your choice, Chet. I'm sure I'll talk to you later." I immediately left and cursed all the way home. I couldn't believe that jackass was trying to cheat me out of my money after I cut him in on the job. But I believed it; even when we worked on BART together, I knew that he was two-faced and would do anything to get more money.

After I calmed down, I said to myself, *"Well, Charlie, you still have some money. Once the club takes off, all this shit won't matter."* I went home and called Joe. I told him what happened and my plans for the club. He offered to front any money that I needed for the club that I could eventually pay back once the club was up and running. I instead made the suggestion that he should become my silent partner. That way, when the club was up and running, he would not only get his money back, but also get a return on it. He liked the idea and agreed. I knew that Joe wouldn't interfere with how I ran things and would help out with any problems, especially since he had an investment in the club.

Once I got off the phone, I called Ann into the bedroom, I guess a little excitedly. She came in running and asking, "What? What?" I said, "Nothing. I just have some stuff to tell you."

She arched her eyebrows, eyed me suspiciously and asked, "What now?"

I said, "Chet doesn't want to give me my commission anymore. I'm going to try and get it, but either way we'll be fine because Joe just agreed to be my silent partner. I'll have the club up and running in no time."

She said, "Okay. As long as the kids and I don't go hungry,

do your thing." We laughed.

She then asked, "Do you know what you're going to name that club?" A little surprised at the question, I answered, "No; I haven't even thought about it." She said, "Well, a name occurred to me the other day. Why not call it the 'C-Note'?"

I asked, "Why did you think of that?" She replied, "Well, I was talking to mom the other day about how much you love money. She said, 'Yeah, that boy doesn't like anything but hundred dollar bills.'" She continued, "I said, 'Yeah, if ain't a c-note, don't even bother.' Then I thought that might not be too bad of a name for your club because you only want people to come that spend a hundred a night." I said, "You're right. I don't want any broke people up in my club. It's going to be classy."

Ann went to check on the girls and I called Jerry. When he picked up I said, "My wife has come up with a money-making name." He replied, "Charlie? Oh, what is it?" I said, "How do you like the sound of the 'C-Note'? Our ads can say, 'If one's not in your wallet, don't even bother coming.'" He said, "That's cool. We're going to make some money." I said, "Yeah. Oh, by the way, Joe's my silent partner. Now if there are any problems, I have a lot of protection."

Jerry replied, "Congratulations. We are on our way." I said, "Yeah, the club should be open in late April or early May."

Time flew by as I prepared the club. With Joe's financial support, money was not a concern. Leroy made sure I had all the paperwork and necessary licenses. The remodeling job was underway and everyone was preparing for the opening day.

While the preparations for the club were in full swing, I still maintained contact with Chet. Chet didn't pay me my commission from March 16. Throughout March and most of April, I still did not receive a dime. He refused to give me any money until I paid the bills. I reminded him that he owed me over $300,000 in commissions. He didn't budge and neither did I. The cleanup job continued while I prepared to open the "C-Note." I still followed the progress of the oil spill and calculated how much I was owed every few days.

March passed uneventfully while preparations continued. By the end of March, Chet owed me $800,000 in back commissions. On Thursday, April 13, 1971, I planned to call Chet and remind him of how much he owed me when he unexpectedly called me.

The phone rang at 7 a.m. and Ann woke me up and said, "Charlie, it's for you." I picked up and said, "Yes. Who is this?" "It's me, Chet. Charlie, I just wanted to let you know that the job is done. Stinson Beach is cleaned up." "The job is completely finished?" "Yeah. Now Standard Oil is just trying to settle all accounts. They really want you to pay the hundred grand, Charlie." "Why don't you pay me the eight hundred grand you owe me, Chet?" "Charlie, we've been through this already. You know the deal."

"Yeah, Chester, I do. And you already know where I stand on the matter." "Fine Charlie. However, if I were you, I'd rethink my position." "Why do you say that?" "Standard Oil always balances their books. Always."

"Is that a threat?" "No, Charlie. Just know that Standard Oil always gets its money or some type of compensation. Always." "Yeah, thanks for the insight. However, I'll just hold onto my money until you get your ass off what's rightfully mine."

I hung up the phone and thought about what Chet had said. I knew Standard Oil was pissed that I still had that money. But I didn't know what they would do. I hadn't heard anything from those cops who pulled me over and threatened me, so I assumed that Standard Oil told the San Francisco Police Department to back off. The club would be opening soon and I was ready to finally put all this crap behind me. However, I couldn't shake the thought that maybe Standard Oil wasn't done with me yet. I kept thinking, "If Tennat can get the police to do his bidding, what will he stoop to next?"

# History 14

# "C-Note"

Despite the concerns nagging me in the back of my mind, the "C-Note" was set to open on Friday, April 28. My house was continually buzzing as people came in and out informing me of plans, and to get my okay on finishing details on the preparations. On April 19, a week and a half before opening night, I was just getting ready to start running ads to increase the mounting hype about the club. However, I received an unexpected visit.

I was proofing the club flyers early that morning when someone began to ring the doorbell incessantly. It was 9 a.m. and I wondered who was at the door. I went downstairs in my robe and looked out the living room window. To my surprise, I saw two cops fidgeting impatiently as they waited for me to answer the door.

I opened the door, stepped outside and closed the door behind me while saying, "Hello gentlemen. What can I do for you?" The short, sunburned cop said rudely, "Charlie Walker?" I answered, "Yes." He continued, "We have a search warrant. Let us in." I said, "What? Let me see your badges and the warrant." They threw their badges in my face and then shoved the warrant in front of my eyes. I snatched and read it. I looked at the allegation: income tax evasion. I asked, "Who can I thank for this?" The tall one gave me a sickly sweet smile and said, "Care of the San Francisco Police

Department." I knew that the city of San Francisco, the San Francisco Police Department and Standard Oil were one and the same. I immediately thought, *"So this is how Tennat wants to proceed now."*

Though only two cops talked to me, I saw three police cars parked along the curb with several other officers getting out wearing gloves and carrying bags. The short cop said, "This shouldn't take too long." He was surprisingly right. I was amazed at how quickly they turned my home into a mess. The cops opened every drawer, threw things on the floor and took out papers, receipts and other random items in large garbage bags.

When they left, my house looked like it had been broken into and vandalized. While the cops were pulling off, Ann returned from her mother's and asked me why there were so many cops on our block. I was standing in the doorway and blocked her view of the living room. When she asked that question, I simply stood aside and let her see what they had done to our home.

When Ann saw the state of the living room, she ran into the house and looked into every room. I still stood in the doorway. After she looked in every room, she came back to me wide-eyed and in shock. She looked dazed and I asked if she was all right. She looked at me, pointed at the living room and whispered, "My house. Look at my house."

She still looked shocked and I really got worried. I pulled her close to me and looked her dead in the eyes while saying, "Ann, we'll clean it up. They're gone now. Don't worry." She then asked, "Why did they do this?" I told her what the cops said and listed most of the charges printed on the warrant. Ann said, "Those bastards. Come on, let's fix up our house."

We went inside and cleaned the house for over two hours. After the house was cleaned, I called Jerry. I told him what happened and we both agreed to postpone the opening of the club until we knew what was going to happen. I then called Joe and Leroy and told them the same. They also agreed to postpone the club opening. Joe said that if any charges were filed, he'd fly up and help me take care of it. I thanked him and hung up. I was concerned because I didn't know what would come of that police search. I called the police department to find out what was going on and what I could expect. A receptionist answered and said, "SFPD. How may I help you?" I answered, "Some officers just searched my house with a warrant. What's going to happen next?" She asked, "Can I have your name?" I said, "Can you just tell me the status of my file or case or whatever it is?" After a moment's hesitation she again asked, "Can I have your name to see if I have any information?" I replied, "Charlie Walker." She sat mute for a few seconds and then said, "Oh... well, I'll have someone get back to you Mr. Walker. Thank you for calling." I said, "Sure," and she abruptly hung up the phone.

After her strange reaction to my name, I knew something was definitely up and that I was in for some legal bullshit. Sure enough, a few days later the same two cops came to my house while I was eating dinner. I knew it was the same ones because they were the only people that incessantly rang my doorbell.

I answered the door and said, "Hi, how can..." I was interrupted by the short cop who said, "Mr. Walker, we have a warrant for your arrest on the charge of income tax evasion," while his partner got ready to handcuff me. Ann ran downstairs and frantically asked what was going on. The short cop happily said, "Ma'am, we're arresting your husband. If you want to, you can bail him out at the precinct." Right before the cop put on the handcuffs, I asked if I could hug my wife. He shrugged and said okay.

I hugged Ann and whispered in her ear, "Call Jerry and Joe." I was immediately handcuffed and led away. Ann must have instantly called Jerry and Joe because Jerry met me at the precinct with a bail bondsman with a blank check in hand. My bail was set at one hundred grand and Jerry put up his house for me. I got home just in time to kiss my girls before they went to bed.

My arraignment was set for the following Monday morning at 10 a.m. sharp. Joe flew up that night and arrived at the house around 2 a.m.. Jerry and Joe stayed at the house the rest of the week. Joe recommended a lawyer who immediately got to work. I would have used Leroy, but he was involved in too many of my activities. He had what is called a conflict of interest. The lawyer Joe suggested came highly recommended; his name was Greg Thomas. Joe, Jerry and I met with Greg and had him spell out all the bullshit. Greg simply said, "Don't worry until we see what they bring at the arraignment."

Ordinarily, such a brief statement would have made me say, "What the fuck does that mean?" However, Greg's composure and confidence assured me that I didn't need to worry just yet.

I spent the rest of the week preparing for my arraignment, reassuring Ann and explaining what I could to my girls because the media was already on my trail and making me look like an urban criminal. Monday came and Ann drove me to the courthouse. Ann, Jerry and Joe sat right behind me during the entire proceedings. Surprisingly enough, I recognized a Standard Oil executive trying to be incognito while sitting in the back row behind the District Attorney. My arraignment was very quick. The proceedings began and Greg immediately asked the judge that all charges be dropped because of insufficient evidence.

The District Attorney interrupted and said, "Your honor, I believe that Mr. Walker is a highly organized lawbreaker and all of his crimes need to be brought to justice. The search warrant gave us just what my office believes to be the tip off the iceberg. Only through a jury trial can we fully show the full range of his crimes." After some more comments from both my attorney and the District Attorney and a brief deliberation, the judge looked at the papers on his desk and replied, "Well, based on your evidence, the case will go to trial. Trial is set for the third Monday in June. Court adjourned." Ann, Joe and Jerry huddled around Greg and me. Greg suggested that we go to his office to have a conversation.

At his office, Greg explained that the charges were filed because I allegedly misreported my earnings on my 1970 income tax return. The crux of the prosecution's argument was that I didn't report all of the income I received once I entered the trucking industry. However, I gave a lot of money away to people in the community to help uplift Hunters Point and share my newfound success.

I explained all of this to Greg and asked, "So, can I beat this?" He said, "Charlie, I think so. Their evidence isn't that strong. We'll have a great chance if you give great testimony." I said, "If that's the case, then I have no worries."

After the arraignment, Joe decided to stay with his sister in Danville during the trial. I told him to just visit periodically. However, he insisted on seeing me through this mess. I reluctantly accepted as long as he promised not to let his business slip in the meantime. Jerry lived close by, but I had a special nook set aside for him to stay as long as was necessary at any given time. With my friends and family behind me, I prepared for my federal trial.

I decided to lie low before and throughout my trial. Even if I had chosen otherwise, I wouldn't have had a choice once the media circus began. Once the media caught wind of my story, it immediately began to portray me as an evil, money-hungry monster. I would make jokes with my daughters about the things the media said. One media report that I watched with Ann and the girls said that I was a smooth criminal.

Landi began to laugh and said, "Charlie, you're not smooth! What are they talking about?" I laughed and said, "I don't know. Those people are crazy." I constantly immersed my family in humor to keep our home life pleasant and as separate from the media frenzy as possible. I had the girls stay with Rudy once they were out of school. My daughters never saw the courthouse during my trial. I also gradually began to watch the news less and less until I stopped. Once the trial began, I only read newspapers; I got tired of seeing my face on the television.

My three-week long trial began as intended on the third Monday in June. I wore my best black suit and sat in my seat calm and collected. Greg had told me that it was important to look concerned, but not afraid. I told him, "Just tell me the face and I'll be wearing it come Monday."

That's what I did. I kept the same expression throughout my trial. Day after day I listened to the prosecution talk about my financial activities and continually ask, "Where did the money go?" By the time the prosecution concluded, I was ready for Greg to rip its argument apart.

Greg's opening comments were something like, "Charlie Walker is not what the prosecution says he is. They say he's a criminal, a mobster, a thief and a cold-hearted man, but they are wrong. Charlie Walker is a husband, a loving and doting father, a businessman and a hero in the black community. Charlie Walker should not be on trial for his actions, he should be applauded..."

During my defense, Greg called various people from the community to testify about how I helped them and the community. Several black truckers testified that my one-man demonstration, and all the expenses that I incurred as a result, gave them the ability to provide for their families. A couple of them even testified that without my help, they would have lost their homes. However, the most poignant testimony came from Leroy, who testified that the money I gave him helped him offer free legal services to poor blacks. When he said that, I saw that the jury was moved.

Greg continued my defense and concluded it with a strong closing statement. The days of my trial soon blurred into monotony and I kept myself occupied with Ann and the girls. I used the trial to relax and regroup in order to prepare for my club opening when it was all over.

After closing statements on both sides, the jury went out to deliberate. They were only out for one day. The previous night, I passed the time watching movies with Ann and the girls.

I didn't know what was coming the next morning and I cherished every fleeting moment with my family. As Ann drove me to the courthouse the following morning, the entire trial flashed through my mind. The trial had lasted for several weeks. It was now early July. I remember how my club was supposed to have opened over a month ago. I simply had to accept that I did not lead my life, but life led me.

I wondered what I would tell my girls if I were found guilty. I knew my girls looked up to me and I didn't want them to think I was the bad man the media made me look like. How would I take care of the girls and Ann from prison? Too many thoughts ran through my mind and I took a deep breath and leaned back in my seat. Ann and I did not say a word during the entire drive. I just massaged her shoulder while I thought. I imagined being in prison and not being able to touch my wife as I was doing just then. I resolved to try and be optimistic and prayed in my heart that Allah was with me.

After Ann parked and we both got out of the car, I said to Ann, "When we leave here, wanna go for some ice cream?" She said, "I'll take you anywhere after this," and smiled. Through her smile I saw her worries deep in her eyes. I just thought, *"Man, what have I put this woman through?"*

Ann must have sensed my thoughts because she said, "Charlie, I like you just the way you are. Now, if you ever think about changing, I'll have to rethink my position." We laughed and walked to the entrance. The media instantly overwhelmed us. I felt the hundreds of cameras surrounding me and quickly pushed my way through them and into the courtroom, which was packed with more reporters and several of Standard Oil's highest executives including Tennat. After I took my seat, I looked back at him and he gave a sardonic smile. I subtly gave him the finger while gently scratching my nose.

My heart was beating so fast that I thought I was going to have a heart attack when I saw the jury slowly walk into the room. My mouth suddenly became dry and I was in dire need of some water to revitalize my nerve-racked body. It only took them a few minutes to sit down and for the foreman to read the verdict. However, it felt like an eternity. I watched the proceedings in slow motion. I noticed the foreman had large sweat stains under his arms and appeared to be nervous. Now that made me nervous. I watched his mouth as he slowly said, "We, the jury, find..."

I strained my head to hear his words.

"...the defendant, Charlie Walker..."

I unconsciously stopped breathing.

"...not guilty."

I deeply exhaled and looked over my shoulder at Ann who had tears of joy in her eyes. Out of the corner of my eye I also saw the disappointed and frustrated expressions on the Standard Oil executives' faces. I smiled to them and waved. I thought to myself, "July 19 will from now on be a holiday for me."

After the judge said, "Mr. Walker, you are free to go. This court is adjourned," I shook my lawyer's hand and hurried over to Ann. I hugged and kissed her and she said, "Let's get that ice cream." I replied, "Only if you're treating." She said, "Sure. I'll be your sugar mama." We laughed while Jerry and Joe walked toward us. I hugged both of them and told them to meet me at the house later to discuss my future plans over drinks.

I picked up the plans for the club and evaluated what still needed to be done; I hadn't looked at them since the trial began. The club was surprisingly close to completion. It just needed a few more decorations and I needed to finish hiring the staff. I discussed the final details with Jerry and Joe, or at least I tried.

When Jerry and Joe arrived, they were ready to celebrate and get drunk. They didn't seem that interested in hearing my plans; in fact, they blew them off. They told me to let the game go for just a night and to kick back and enjoy my triumphant day. I thought they were acting a little strange, but I figured I might as well relax.

A few days after my acquittal, Ann told me she had a surprise for me. It was a Saturday afternoon and she refused to tell me what it was and just told me to be dressed in my best suit by 9 p.m.. She then took the girls to Rudy's so they couldn't spoil the surprise. Ann knew full and well that I could get my girls to tell me anything.

I spent the day going over the club plans, checking on my finances and talking to my brothers; I updated them on my future plans. At 9 p.m. sharp, I was dressed to kill. I had on my navy blue suit, which accentuated my muscular frame. My hair was freshly cut and my shoes shined brightly. Ann wore a beautiful black dress and looked very lovely. I asked her where we were going.

She said, "Don't worry about it, but I do have to blindfold you." Shocked, I asked, "Why?" She answered, "Because silly, it's a surprise. You know this city inside and out. I don't want you to figure it out."

I let my wife blindfold me and drive my Cad to some unknown destination. We drove for about fifteen minutes when Ann abruptly stopped. She parked, helped me out of my seat and led me - still blindfolded - to her surprise. After walking what seemed like a few feet, I heard the faint sound of music. As we continued to walk, the previously faint music became louder and louder. By that time, I thought I had figured out the surprise. Ann obviously had taken me to a party. Well, I was partially right.

We abruptly stopped and Ann said, "We're here." She then promptly took off my blindfold and said, "Look." I opened my eyes and saw that we were in front of my club, which apparently was open because I could see a party going on behind the bouncer and there was a long line of people waiting to get in. I stood amazed as I saw "The C-Note" in big, bold, black letters. Under the sign, a big banner read, "Grand Opening."

I continued to stare dumbfounded around me, so Ann nudged

me and said, "Let's go in." We walked in and I immediately heard cheers from the entire crowd. All of my friends, employees and different people from the neighborhood were there having a grand time. A big banner on a wall read, "Welcome Back, Charlie." I spotted Jerry, who was having drinks with a couple of girls. I also saw Joe sitting at a table with Frank and Lileo. I walked around, and spoke to everybody.

After I greeted everyone, someone randomly yelled, "Speech!" Apparently the crowd agreed because everyone began to chant, "Speech, Speech." The deejay stopped playing the music and everyone stared at me expectantly. I took a deep breath and walked to the front of the dance floor.

I said, "I still can't believe all of you guys did this. I'm glad that all of my real friends are here to share this day with me. I just want to say I'm not going anywhere; Charlie is here to stay!"

My little speech was received with cheers and clapping. The deejay started playing music and people began to dance again. It looked like my club was going to be a big hit. I found Ann sitting with Jerry's wife, Nancy. I gave Ann a kiss and then sat down with Joe and Jerry. I asked them how did they make it happen. Joe said, "Since the club was practically finished, we decided to get it ready so that if you were acquitted, you wouldn't have to deal with that minor stuff." Jerry added, "We knew that having a party soon after your trial would draw a huge crowd because of all the publicity. So, how do you like your hit?"

I said, "This is crazy! How much did we make tonight?" Jerry said, "Let's just say, the drinks are on us." We laughed and toasted to our newfound success.

I ran the nightclub for three years until some arsonists burned it down; they were never identified. I used the insurance money to get back in the trucking business. My life quieted down somewhat, but I remained a hero to many blacks, gained some respect with some open-minded whites, and even prominence in certain circles in San Francisco. I stayed involved in the black community and tried to help out the brothers whenever I could. I finally settled into my comfortable old life filled with my family, trucking and, of course, the occasional party.

•   •   •

My spirit was relaxed. There was a strong degree of comfort and an attitude of letting bygones be bygones. But what I did not know at the time was that there was still a continuous movement against me. I was prey to those who were yet hunting me for my livelihood and perhaps, my very blood.

"Now, if you ever think about changing,
I'll have to rethink my position"

# History 15

# "After Five Year"

$F$ive years had passed since I worked for Standard Oil. The year was 1976 and I was in the hauling business and back in the game. I was even working with Chet again. Good businessmen didn't get mad; they got even. My life stabilized back into the comfortable lifestyle that I created for myself after I started working on BART. Standard Oil was a distant bad memory, pushed far into the recesses of my mind.

My re-entry into trucking was like a new beginning and I felt the thrill of unlimited possibilities lying before me.

One day in October, I vaguely heard the doorbell ring from my room. I yelled, "Dee Dee, answer that!" After a few seconds, she yelled back, "Charlie, please come down here."Her voice, normally lively and full, was now softer and she sounded a bit frightened.

I could always tell when something was wrong with my girls and I bounded down the stairs to see what was wrong. I walked to the front door and saw Dee Dee's confused expression. I moved her aside and then turned my attention to whoever was at the door.

I looked out the door and saw two police officers holding a search warrant. I immediately felt déjà vu from the time when my federal trial had started. However, I pushed that thought out of my mind because I hadn't done anything wrong and I had already been tried once for all that Standard Oil crap. I told my daughter to go upstairs and to gather her sisters and stay in their room. She looked scared and perplexed. I told her that I had everything under control. A look of relief immediately ran across her face and she hopped upstairs somewhat lighthearted.

Once she left, the first officer said, "Are you Mr. Walker?"

I replied, "Yes." He continued, "I'm Officer Lee and this is my partner, Officer Johnson. We have a warrant to search your house. Please cooperate with us and we'll get this done as soon as we can, sir."

His polite attitude calmed me down somewhat and I asked to look at the search warrant. The search warrant said they were going to search my house on suspicion of twenty-six felony charges including state income tax invasion - the very charge I had been acquitted of in my federal trial.

I looked at him and said, "How can this be? I was already tried and acquitted for this stuff."

He looked a little confused and said, "Well, I don't know. You probably want to talk to your lawyer. Now, we are going to proceed." As he said that, more policemen emerged from the three squad cars parked by the curb. They wore gloves and carried the now all-too-familiar garbage bags that I recalled from the first search. I went upstairs and talked to my girls. I told them that the police were searching our house because they had nothing better to do. I then told them to go to their grandmother's. Ann was out running errands at the time. I called Rudy and had her come over right away. She then took the girls to her place. I couldn't drive them myself because I wanted to watch the police and make sure that they didn't try and pull anything funny. They were not going to plant anything in my house!

After an hour and a half, they left with numerous garbage bags and my house ripped to shreds. I cleaned up immediately because I didn't want Ann to see the house destroyed again. I finished just in time. As I was putting the last shirt in its drawer, I heard Ann run upstairs. She immediately asked where were the girls. I replied, "They are at Rudy's."

She asked, "Why?"

I said, "Because we had police visitors with a search warrant." She said, "But look at the house, did they really search it?" I answered, "Yeah, I just cleaned it up before you got back." "Well, what did they want, Charlie?"

"Who knows? The warrant had the same charge I beat in my trial and a host of others. This smells like some bad bullshit and I'm going to find out what's going on." I went upstairs and called Jerry. I told him what happened and we were both stumped. He suggested that I call my old lawyer, Greg, and find out what was up as soon as possible. I agreed and instantly called him. After his receptionist transferred me to his private line and announced me, Greg said, "Charlie, what can I do for you?" I replied, "I don't know what's going on, but I need you to find out. The police came by my house with another search warrant today. The charge was the same as the one I beat in federal court. How can they do that?" He said, "I don't know. Let's wait and see if they file charges."

I answered, "You can wait. I'm going to see what I can find out." I made a call back to Jerry just to let him know what was happening. I told him to keep an ear out for any news that might come his way. I called the police department, but I couldn't get through to anyone. The receptionist took my message and rudely hung up the phone. I thought, *"I guess some things will never change."*

I spent the rest of the night wondering what was happening. I had settled into my life and didn't need any bullshit from the past trying to shake up things. I talked to Ann, Rudy and the girls and reassured them that everything was going to be okay. They had faith in my ability to handle situations and I needed them to be calm and trusting while I figured this out.

Three days later, two officers came to arrest me on charges of state income tax evasion, falsification of corporate records, perjury and the list went on and on.

When the officer reading the charges got halfway done, I asked him, "Can you just give me a list of all the charges and arrest me already? This is taking too long."

He insisted on reading all twenty-six charges and doing everything by the book. Both officers were clear, direct and brief. I wasn't surprised and Ann immediately called Jerry, Joe and Greg. Jerry wanted to bail me out, but this time my bail was set at $500,000. Joe flew up and immediately bailed me out. That night I met with Joe and Jerry. I said, "I am too old for this shit. I keep getting déjà vu because this seems exactly like what I went through with my federal trial. I don't want to go through this crap again, but those bastards are ruthless." Joe said, "Don't those bastards ever quit?" I said, "No. Not until they get money, blood or both."

Greg called me the following day and said that my arraignment was set for the following Wednesday. He told me to remain calm until I knew what was happening and I did. On Wednesday morning, Ann drove me to the courthouse just like she had five years earlier. Once the proceedings began, Greg asked that my tax evasion charge be dismissed based on lack of evidence and the fact that I was acquitted of it already. The prosecution keenly reminded him that my new charge was income tax evasion on my 1971 tax returns from the year I worked for Standard Oil. The judge quickly said that there was sufficient evidence for all twenty-six charges to go to trial, which was set for the second Monday in November.

Greg wanted to talk to me after my arraignment, but I went home and went to sleep. I had an excruciatingly painful headache. I avoided all calls and watched television with my girls. During that time, I was trying to figure out what scenario was playing out and how I could beat it. I didn't put everything together, but by the end of the night, I knew Standard Oil was behind it all.

The following morning, while I was eating breakfast, Greg called me. The way he said, "Charlie, let's meet now," let me know that I was in for it. I replied, "Okay. I'll be in your office in a half hour."

When I entered Greg's office, his face was grave. He quietly said, "Sit down," while gathering his words carefully. I said, "Man, if you don't say something soon, I'm going to go crazy." He simply said, "Charlie, they've got you."

I asked, "Who?"

He said, "Standard Oil. I don't know how they've done it, but they've managed to make it look like you've stolen over a hundred grand from them. They are out to get you and they want blood. This entire case is bullshit, but they've bought everyone on this. Even if you spend all of your money, I don't know if you can beat it."

"I didn't give Chet that one-hundred grand because he wouldn't give me my commission. Standard Oil and Chet Smith owe me over $800,000. Can I sue them?" "Not without the SFPD and court system behind you."

I asked, "Are you telling me that they have me out-and-out? What kind of time am I looking at?" "Up to eight years in Folsom, the hardest place around." "Well Greg, what are my options?" "Spend all your money and hope that it works or sit back and let time run its course."

After Greg said that, I just got up and walked out. I didn't know what to do. I couldn't believe those bastards at Standard Oil were still after me. Those vengeful assholes waited five years to come and get me! Whatever was going to happen, I was not going to lose all the money I had worked so hard to get. I resolved within myself that if they had to have a piece of me, that was fine, but they were never going to see any of my money.

I drove home and wondered how I would handle the trial that I knew was coming. At least my mother, Rudy, Ann and the girls would be taken care of financially. I had all of my money at their disposal and if worst came to worst, Joe would help with whatever else they needed. I went and called Ann and my girls into my room and told them the deal - all of it. I said that Standard Oil was still after me and this time they had me. However, I assured them that they would all be taken care of and once they got me, it would finally be over. Ann and the girls became upset and a little hysterical at the thought of me going to jail. I purposely had not used the word "prison." I told them to calm down and think about the situation. I said that this was all business. Standard Oil wanted me so bad that I would give them a piece of me. I would just make sure they only got a piece and that my family would be financially set. I spent the evening with my family to reassure them and just to spend some quality time with them because I knew that those precious moments weren't guaranteed to me anymore.

The following week, I met with Greg and thanked him for all of his help. I also said that I wasn't going to keep him as my attorney. I knew what was coming and I prepared to save my money rather than go to jail and go broke from lawyers' fees. I decided to use the court-appointed attorney because I knew what was coming and a high-priced attorney wasn't going to stop it. After I came to terms with the situation, I just sat back and let Standard Oil come for me.

My trial didn't actually start until late November. The prosecution started out with the big guns by calling me all types of names and a horrible criminal. The media had a field day with my new trial. They had already tried to run my name through the mud during my previous trial. Whites and blacks alike thought I was a criminal, but I didn't mind. I understood that blacks didn't understand capitalism and how it really worked. As for whites, well, I didn't expect anything more from them. Imagine: a black man in business who was not a criminal! To the average white person, the idea must have been preposterous. If the media wanted to call me a criminal, that was fine, but then every other businessman in America was also a criminal.

My attorney was a young, enthusiastic white boy who wanted to beat my charges. He fully believed in the law and was fresh out of law school. He couldn't understand why I was so apathetic about the proceedings. I didn't even bother explaining my situation to him; we were lifetimes apart and he would have never understood my situation.

In any event, my trial lasted a previously unheard-of four months. The prosecution bombarded the jury with so-called evidence of my life of crime. After looking at those twelve pale faces once, I knew that I was on my way to jail.

I never really considered what jail would mean to me. Intellectually, I understood what it meant to lose my freedom, but I couldn't emotionally grasp what effect that would have on me. I pushed those types of thoughts aside and focused on keeping my family secure.

During my trial, I found the prosecution's argument quite funny. They took one tiny piece of evidence and tried to create a large and grand argument from it. For instance, the prosecution spent about one day alone on the blank truck tags that I signed when working at Stinson Beach. They said that because of those tags, I was an embezzler, committed grand theft and did other things. My only question for the prosecution, which I never got to ask, was if those blank truck tags were such a big deal, why was I, the only black person, on trial for using them when numerous other executives signed off on them too. I had to stifle laughs all through that argument, especially when I reflected that I first used those blank truck tags to get the big wheels some coke and girls.

As my trial progressed, I became increasingly sure of my fate. However, a degree of comfort also rose within me because I knew that my family would be provided for. As the months came to a close and the jury left to deliberate my fate, my family began to accept what was about to transpire. Though my girls never accepted that I should go to jail, they knew that if I did go, I would still take care of them. Ann and I talked and she said she worried about the girls and me. It took me longer to reassure her, but with Rudy's help, she too came to accept the inevitable.

On a cold February Tuesday morning, I received a phone call that the jury was back with a verdict after about a week of deliberating. Ann and I immediately drove to the courthouse. Jerry met us inside the courtroom. I waited patiently as the foreman read the verdict. "We the jury, find the defendant, Charlie Walker, guilty of..." I immediately said to my attorney, "Told you," and waited for the foreman to finish reading all that I was found guilty of. In total, I was convicted on three charges: extortion, grand theft and state income tax evasion.

Two weeks later, I was sentenced to six years in Folsom State Prison and immediately hauled away in handcuffs. As I sat in my jail cell, I wondered what prison would be like. Ann and my girls came to visit me before they sent me away; they were upset and sad. I guess they hoped that somehow I would get off, but after I reassured them that everything would be okay and that Folsom was just temporary, they were alright. My family always had an unshakeable faith in me that even prison couldn't destroy.

The following morning, I was transferred to Folsom State Prison. I arrived at 10:30 a.m.. While I was being processed, I was shackled to the other prisoners. Throughout my trial, I had tried to accept the idea of prison, but when it actually happened, it was still a shock and I had to adjust to it. I kept my eyes open and tried to learn as much as I could about the place. The guards, all white, walked between us, never saying a word. They sneered at us, trying to intimidate us, but I saw right through them because I knew what to expect from them, and how to deal with their mindset. There were ten blacks including myself, three whites, and three Mexicans being processed. In the background loomed a large yard about the size of a football field and a huge building that looked deserted against the gray sky. Lights flickered from the gun towers in all corners of the

182

building. All time seemed to stop as I waited to be processed. At fifty years old, I had received my first jolt. I later learned that I was the only black white-collar criminal in all of Folsom. All the other people, rather prisoners, were there for murder, robbery, drug sales, kidnapping, rape and other serious crimes.

Every prisoner read the newspaper and my case was highly publicized. The California Department of Corrections officers and all the prisoners knew me. I was alone in a cell with one sheet and one blanket, a mattress and a steel frame bunk attached to the concrete wall, and a steel toilet bowl with no cover sat in the corner. Seated on the side of the steel bunk, I put my head in my hands and started to think. My mind still could not comprehend the reality of the situation. I had never been confined except when I was in the Air Force in Alaska. Of course, I was much younger then. I ran away from home when I was fifteen and joined the Air Force. I was the same size at fifteen as I was in Folsom; I was always large for my age. In retrospect, prison and the Air Force were somewhat alike. I had known numerous men who had been in jail and prison and my secret desire had always been to see the inside of a prison.

I lifted my head and said to myself, *"Well Charlie, you are fifty years old. You have great children, a mother, a wife, a home about paid for and many memories, but this is a new experience."*

I spent the day wondering, *"How in the hell did I get here?"*

I reflected on my life and all of my decisions. I had plenty of time to think about all the mistakes I had made in my life. Unquestionably, the best decision I made was marrying Ann; all the rest were so-so. I kept thinking about Ann and all the bullshit I took her through.

It was difficult to look around and only see bars, but I reminded myself that this was only temporary. The first day, I had a good talk with myself and swore that I would make the best of my time in Folsom. Even though I was in prison, I still beat Standard Oil. They took my freedom for a while, but they would never see that money again.

On my second day, I went to the yard for the first time. As I walked down the steps leading to the yard, I saw that the prisoners were segregated by race. I saw the black prisoners were on the left, Mexicans were over by the handball court and whites were directly in front of me. I immediately walked toward the black prisoners. As I was approaching, a prisoner said, "Charlie, my brother, am I glad to see you! Are you okay?" I said, "Yes." While I was standing, about thirty or forty prisoners approached me asking, "Are you Charlie Walker?" while shaking my hand. I replied, "Yes." All of them said, "Right on brother! Glad to meet you. If anyone bothers you, let me know."

This continued for an hour. All the blacks wanted to meet me and one young brother brought me a pint of ice cream. Another one brought me a soft drink. One brother said, "All my guys are with you if you have any problems."

I was amazed at the prisoners' actions; I didn't know what to expect. They were very friendly to me and respected all that I had done on the outside. They also knew that my conviction was bull-shit. I walked around the track with a line of inmates following me, asking, "How was it on the outside? How much time did you get?" I answered, "Six years." A prisoner said, "There is no justice in this country. I know some white guy that killed two people and didn't get as much time as you did. You didn't kill anybody." I said, "That is the price you pay if you are black in America."

Then another brother asked, "Say man, can you play pinochle?" I replied, "No." He said, "Brother, that is the game. You have got to learn it; I'll teach you." I said, "Okay."

It took me several days to learn the game. By the end of the week, I was playing like a pro and had settled into my current situation. The other prisoners were surprised by my consistent composure. Most guys that came in would freak out over losing their freedom and being caged up. What they didn't know was that I knew I would be in Folsom long before I arrived. It wasn't easy being locked up, but I did what I had to make sure my family was taken care of and to screw over those jerks at Standard Oil. They wanted a piece of me and I let them have it. They took six years of my life, although I'd be out in three for good behavior. However, they never got what they wanted: all the money I got from them. I saw Folsom as a trade-off in which I still won.

After I had been in Folsom for several months and the guards saw how influential I was with the prisoners, I was made the Inmate Recreation Representative. I wasn't surprised that I was chosen out of five hundred prisoners. I had never been in any trouble. Everyone who knew me, black, white or Mexican, respected me. When some of the prisoners were in trouble, I helped by talking to a sergeant or lieutenant. My new position had great perks. I had my own office and a hotplate. I decided to work seven days a week although I was only paid for five; it helped pass the time more quickly. No one complained about my free labor either.

As time progressed, the days and weeks passed more quickly. I tried not to think about the future too much, but rather just enjoyed my vacation - that was how I viewed Folsom. It was like a mandatory vacation and I didn't plan on stressing myself out with unnecessary worries.

Ann and the girls visited me every weekend. It was hard when they left because I would feel lonely, but I liked seeing them and still being a part of their lives. They were initially worried about me, but when they saw me hanging out with the other inmates and playing cards, they knew I was alright. My family and I were very calm during my time at Folsom because we knew it was temporary. It was something we had to endure for a short while to keep what those jackasses kept trying to take away from me.

My time in Folsom was over relatively soon in my mind. I was out in three years because one day was removed from my sentence for every day that I worked.

The years passed, only marked by different holiday decorations that changed every other month. My life became a consistent routine, something I had avoided all of my life. However, my release date came before I knew it.

On the day of my release, a guard walked up and said, "Walker!" I replied, "Yes?" He said, "Get your stuff together. You're leaving." I said, "What?" He said, "You're being released today. Now hurry up." I quickly calculated the time in my head and arrived at roughly three years. I replied, "Okay."

My cell door opened and I walked out with my few belongings. While I was walking down my tier, some prisoners asked where I was going. I said that I was being released. The prisoners began to cheer and say congratulations as I walked past their cells. I felt grateful that the prisoners, many who would never be on the outside again, were happy for me. I waved goodbye before walking down the stairs leading to the exit.

At the front gate, my wife and girls greeted me with hugs and kisses. They had rented a limousine to drive me home triumphantly. In the limousine, I reclined and relaxed while taking in the fresh air. I was proud that I had survived my time in Folsom and that my family was still together.

The limousine dropped us off at the house and Jerry greeted me outside. Rudy had fixed her special fried chicken just for me and we had a very small dinner party with my family and Jerry. After dinner, Jerry and I sat to talk about my future plans. Jerry said, "Charlie, what are you going to do?" I replied, "I want to go back into trucking. Are my trucks okay?" "Well, they're okay; just a little rusty. How do you plan on getting started?" I asked, "Are there any big jobs going on?" Jerry answered, "Well, there's some construction going on downtown." I said, "Well there it is. If there's any piece of a job left, it'll be mine tomorrow." Jerry congratulated me on my release and on starting my business again. I told him, "Thanks. This time things are going to go my way." Jerry soon left and I went to bed, very exhausted.

Before I could fall asleep, my girls ran into my room and jumped in the bed. Landi explained, "We're going to sleep all together tonight, as one big family." I said, "Okay," and Ann got in last.

We barely fit in that bed, so we snuggled really close to each other. I watched the rest of them sleep peacefully. I thought, *"It feels really good to be home."* With that thought, I finally went to sleep. The following morning I woke up at 7 and left at 8 to go downtown and start trucking all over again.

# Law of the Jungle